HUNT FOR THE FALLEN

FALLEN

TRANSPORT BOOK TWO

HUNT FOR THE FALLEN

TRANSPORT BOOK TWO

Peter Welmerink

 SEVENTH STAR PRESS

Cover art: Jason C. Conley
Cover art in this book copyright © 2014 Jason C. Conley & Seventh Star
Press, LLC.

Interior Illustrations Tim Holtrop
Interior illustrations © 2014 Tim Holtrop
www.timholtrop.com

Editor: Rodney Carlstrom

Published by Seventh Star Press, LLC.

ISBN Number: 978-1-941706-19-0

Seventh Star Press
www.seventhstarpress.com
info@seventhstarpress.com

Publisher's Note:
Hunt for the Fallen is a work of fiction. All names, characters, and places
are the product of the author's imagination, used in fictitious manner.
Any resemblances to actual persons, places, locales, events, etc. are purely
coincidental.

Printed in the United States of America

First Edition

Acknowledgements

I would like to acknowledge my family for being there, either in the background giving me time to tap at the keyboard, or listening to me try to explain what is this story I am trying to tell.

Special thanks to Ken Campbell, Jason Conley, Tim Holtrop, Tyson Mauermann, Tim Marquitz, Steven Shrewsbury, Stephen Zimmer, Mark Kahn and my editor Rodney Carlstrom.

And a very special thanks again to you, Grand Rapids. Growing up within your embrace, I found adventure, both real and fictional. The fictional stuff makes for more fun reading, so I'll refrain from boring you with the nonfictional stuff...for now. Thank you.

Dedication

This is dedicated to the 1460th Transportation Company based out of Midland, Michigan, who headed back over to Afghanistan in November (2013). Scott, Josh. Proud of you guys and your unit. Looking forward to sitting around a campfire again, having some beers and laughs.
(Note: at time of publication, 1460th was back home. Safe.)

Another WARRIOR I would like to dedicate this book to, my cousin, Lisa Chichester, who fought the good fight against cancer for ten long years. Who remained positive throughout and is an inspiration to us all. Though we lost her in November 2014, her memory lives on and Heaven has a new angel.

BILLET'S BITCH SESSION
Journal Entry - Thursday, April 2, 2026

Yesterday I gunned down a family of three.

Almost to a food delivery point, as spring storms pounded us like Niagara Falls, we neared the DZ blinded by the downpour. Loutonia could hardly see under the poor visibility, and the rest of us were holed up inside. No one saw the guy and gal with a young child in tow step out in front of the transport.

The front wheels crushed them first. The father went halfway under the left rear track. It flattened him below the belt line like a pancake.

If I live to be 100, which I hardly expect, I will never forget the inhuman trill of the undead screaming when surprised and... hurt.

We stopped. Everyone got out: Phelps, Stokes, Mulholland and a couple grunts we were to drop off at the M45 Outpost.

No one knew what to do.

The father and mother—the only thing I could deduce by the way they reached for each other and shrieked when they saw the kid with his skull broke like an egg—called in half the neighborhood. I could tell the glassy-eyed civilians shambling towards us were already agitated by the thunder and lightning storm; the mashed family, screaming as they were, drew the others in like yelling, "dinner's served."

I didn't want to put my crew in any more danger than they were, so I pulled my pistol.

My gun held live rounds, live rounds not allowed in the neighborhood, and I put a bullet in dad, mom and kid's skull.

We could've left them out there. Their own crowded in like crows to roadkill and would have feasted on them, cleaning up the mess.

But I couldn't do that.

I ordered the family picked up and loaded into the Huron. Stokes and Phelps didn't like that and openly voiced their opposition. Stokes whined because he didn't want to get his stumpy little hands dirty, Loutonia because she had cleaned the guts of our rig before we had left.

We arrived back in town. The neighborhood's undead civilians still had living relations in the city. The relatives, along with our higher-ups, were none too happy considering I explained it as a mercy kill. My reasoning was disregarded and we all were fined 250 dead presidents. I got fined a hard-earned grand, including time in the brig. Luckily, the Brass along with a few city commissioners waved the big fine and jail time due to my "heroic endeavors" from last Fall.

Which is a fucking joke. But that's another story.

Feeling guilty, I paid everyone's fines.

Feeling doubly guilty, I didn't sleep worth two shits last night. Visions of the family of three haunted me. A vision of my dead wife and son stood in place of the zombie woman and her boy.

Bonus, we head back out today, usual feeding run and a few more drop offs to the gate outposts. Including a few MP's who are none too happy about it.

It's still raining.

Thunder.

Lightning.

All the good shit that riles both the living and the unliving.

The city weather folk predict ongoing precipitation. Even our Special Operations Weather Technician's say the area is in for some extremely wet days. After the heavy winter and late thaw we've had, both groups are concerned there will be major flooding along the expanse of the Grand River. That's 250 miles of rising river water, coming straight through Grand Rapids.

Hoohah!

Happy Spring.

There are days where I wish for a bullet through the skull.

J.E.B.

Chapter One
In the Urinal of the Gods

"April showers bring watery hell."

Captain Jake Billet walks the perimeter fence, cussing, grumbling. He rings his soaked beret for the umpteenth time. Places it back on his head, knowing it will do little good.

The rain keeps on coming.

On the opposite side of the concertina-crowned fencing: the local undead citizens of Grand Rapids. They are as wet and agitated as he, a sea of tattered clothing on rotting flesh. They groan, snarl, and snap. Broken teeth gnash behind dry blackened lips. Gnarled bony fingers entwine with the chain link separating them from the soldiers standing on the opposite side. The towering city watches anxiously from across the flooded river. The Zees heave at the fence like inmates intent on getting out of their prison. Baleful eyes look upon Billet, they do not see as a friend but perhaps an appetizing foe. They growl at him as if the cause of the storms and constant precipitation is his fault.

"At ease," Jake says as decayed nasal cavities sniff at him as he continues by.

On his side of the enclosure, lining the west bank of the river, the GRCC troops amass. Two immense heavy transport vehicles, his rig, the Huron, and another, the Ontario, stand parked, their back ends toward the enclosure. An Abrams tank and a re-commissioned M-60 Patton from the 44th Street armory, along with a half dozen BRV-O's (Blast Resistant Vehicle-Off Road) span this side of the river border, from Outpost Pearl to Outpost Bridge. The soldiers appear ready for war; the one hundred-plus military men and women line the swollen river bank.

Billet warily eyes the Abrams tank.

"Another grand day, aye Captain?" A young soldier, Wills on his name tape, too cheery, nods at Billet. The GRCC soldier, Gurks as they were called, stands with assault rifle in the crotch of his arm. The orange bottom of the ammunition clip reveals nonlethal rounds, rubber bullets.

Wills loses his cheery demeanor when he sees Billet's sour look.

The sky rumbles.

The Zees slowly stir, angry bees in molasses.

Wills takes up his rifle, stiffens as he tenses.

"They're not coming through, soldier." Billet stops, checks his attitude. He can see the young Private is nervous.

Wills relaxes but keeps rifle in hand.

"It's sure a pleasure to have you in our midst, sir." Wills says, his admiration abundant. "When we're called out to stand guard with the Huron, crew and captain, this crappy weather is hard pressed to get us down."

Billet can't look at Wills. He can't look at the undead civilians, or the other men and women of their unit. He focuses on a decrepit building on the other side of the fence, where the west side of town rots.

He knows why the kid is all a-gush.

Seven months ago they brought a piece of shit to justice. William Lettner stood before his peers and hung for his crimes. The people of Grand Rapids, though the end game had not occurred on their immediate turf, raised hands in celebration. A lakeshore tyrant had been struck down. It was supposed to be a covert op. Names leaked when the job was done. He and his crew were admonished but mainly lauded as heroes. He does not feel like a hero.

Billet didn't know what to say the young soldier. "If we had soap, this would be a fine shower. I'm hoping Command will give the word on next steps they want to go here." He returns his focus on the milling, snarling citizen zombies.

"They're like spooked cattle." Wills jerks his head to discharge the raindrops from the rim of his helmet. "All the storms and heavy rain, I haven't seen them all crowded up like this."

"Too close to the city for anyone's comfort," Billet replies. "If they weren't all packed along the fence here I'm sure we'd be slogging through the neighborhood there," nods towards the inside of the enclosure, the UCRA (Undead Civilian Retention Area). "Our friends in their comfy homes across the river don't want any of their relations to flounder in a puddle and drown."

"I wouldn't want to go trolling inside there even in your big armored box with the civilians so riled." Wills sucks in his breath. "Uh, no offense against your rig, sir."

"At ease, soldier. None taken." Jake agrees with the man's statement though. Normal travel routes through the west side are unsafe at present; the walking cadavers are way too agitated. Still, if they were told to go inside… "Keep tossing in the Z-rations. If City Central thinks this will appease them until the storm breaks, so be it."

Wills grimaces, looks down at the small crate near his muck-covered boots. "I hate that shit. It numbs my hand every time I touch it. They could've given us scoops or something."

"Come on, man. This is prime city factory meat," another young soldier says a few feet away. "A delicious slurry of 'brains-in-a-can,' specially made, laced with whatever sedatives they put in there, yummy doped meat byproduct." The soldier dips her fingers in the open can she holds, comes up with a drippy meat dollop the color of Kentucky clay. The red-brown slop drools down her fingers. She sticks her tongue out, takes a little sample. She chews and purrs like a kitten. "Like good ole Mayor Honeywell says, 'this'll keep our docile and domesticated friends happy, storms or no storms.'"

"Are you turning on us, Private?" Jake says to the other soldier. His brow furrows; his hand moves towards his holstered pistol.

"Uh, sir. No, sir." She says quickly. She spits several times, lets her tongue hang out.

"Feed them, not yourself," Billet says, nodding towards the groaning folk behind the fence. "Mission's to keep our beloved West Side Horde calm until the storms let up and they move back into deeper confines, away from the rising river and City Central inhabitants. So until someone higher up figures out something else…"

"I hope they come up with something soon." Wills lifts a boot. *Shh-lorp.* He reveals soaked and mud-slopped leather. "River gets any higher, we're going swimming. Or they are." He nods towards the Zees.

Jake can't fault the grunts statement there. His eyes scan the perimeter.

The bigger vehicles stay on the roadway and paved trails running along the river between Pearl Street and Bridge Street. The armed footmen stand on sodden earth, grass lawns turned to mud. Between the fence and the troops lies a strip of land slowly being consumed by the rising river. Across the river, on the east side, downtown Grand Rapids and her nervous inhabitants who peer at the rushing, rising waters and a sea of their undead friends congregating on the other side.

Too close. Not good. Billet shakes his head.

He doesn't want to speak his concern out loud, make it any more obvious, and stress the troops any more than they are. He doesn't like it. The storms and heavy, nonstop rainfall have been going on for a solid week, the waterway behind them gurgles at "moderate" flood levels.

So the officials say.

Nine feet above normal is "major" in Jake's book. Surrounding shoreline is gone. The swollen river skims and tickles the underbelly of the bridges at the twenty-one foot mark.

"Two more feet, easy with hundreds of creeks and streams feeding the Grand River," he says under his breath.

And more rainfall to come.

With two more feet, the river comes over the flood walls on the east and west sides, spreads without hindrance into the UCRA where the city's undead wander.

With two more feet.

Billet shakes his head, more to clear the mental image than the rain from his beret. "Command's talking about pushing back the line if the river rises further," Jake says. "Not sure what that will do when you have places downstream they can get into trouble," his eyes on the zombs. "Plus Central hasn't heard from the Butterworth Test Facility. I think there's worry the facility's been compromised. That's a lot of important real estate down the drink." No pun intended.

He is sure the city council is more worried about their beloved UCRA civilians getting loose, coming across the river, and clawing at their doorstep.

The living inner city citizens are damn sure their undead neighbors are taken care of. Afflicted friends and family meander about the west side streets in some mockery of life. They don't deserve to be shot; they don't deserve to be put out of their misery. There are laws so no one can simply walk in and start throwing lead around. There are undead friends and family within the enclosure who, if not nourished with the city's special processed "brains in a can" would not be so "docile and domesticated." Loved ones who would chew your face off if you went to kiss them.

"I know we've been out here for days, Private. I appreciate it, and I'm sure everyone across the river appreciates it." Billet looks down at Wills' rifle. Orange-tipped magazine. Nonlethals like everyone is carrying.

As far as he knows, the Mayor and city council have no clue what they will do if the rains don't abate and the flooding worsens. The bug squirms in his ass—as it does all the troops—standing out here. He doesn't have anything against the poor bastards on the other side of the fence. He and the troops get paid for this duty, but it doesn't mean he has to like it.

Jake's wet tactical vest weighs heavy. His shirt beneath clings tight to his chest, feels like a tightening cocoon. Inside, something else tries to drown his spirit.

Those rotting faces glaring at him squeeze up the vision of his dead wife and son. He plays a cool head, strong heart, nothing fazes him; but the rotters on the other side of the fence...

"If anything, I hope they'll at least give us some dry boots," Wills says, lifting his leg and the muck-covered boot. He flicks it.

A blob of brown slop hits the fence, splits into further pieces of sodden soil. It splatters upon the chest and open mouth of a tottering male Zee on the other side. The necrotized gent works his unhinged jaw as if he's just been tossed a treat. He chews on the ground stew, crunches dirt, grass, small stones; drools out mud, blood and a dislodged tooth.

Wills laughs, but cuts it short, and clears his throat as he notices Billet not reciprocating.

Jake envisions the river engulfing the entire place, zombies stirred to a frantic tizzy. The mud his gnawed flesh.

"Think I'm gonna be sick," the female soldier groans.

"You need me to call a Medic?" Wills asks.

She squats and throws up on her boots.

Wills looks at Billet with a wet frown.

"Hang in there, soldier." *And do your job,* Billet tells himself.

He replaces his frown with a grin, pats Wills on the shoulder and continues his trek towards his vehicle.

The fake humor blows out of Jake as he looks to the big transport several yards away—a rain-blurred rectangular boulder in the distance—he sees a new reason to frown, and curses.

***

"Stokes, what *are* you doing?"

The squat gunner, Sergeant James Stokes, sits on the rear roof of the Huron, one leg hangs over the side. The other leg bent at the knee, pressed to his broad chest; a M4 combat assault rifle nestled in the crotch of his knee and chest. His tanker's helmet sat askew on his head deflecting the relentless rain.

The gunner turns, looks down as his right hand flicks something over the top of the enclosure, over the top of the fence which stands a head lower than the big transports roof line.

"What?" the sergeant tries to sound innocent. His left hand holds an open can of Z-ration. A stumpy half of wet cigar hangs from the corner of his mouth, bounces with every word. It reminds Billet more of a runny dog turd than an actual smoke.

Jake tries to remain calm. It blows out like a stroke of lightning. "What the fuck are you up to?"

"Found an ex-girlfriend. Just having some fun with her."

Billet groans, rolls his eyes. He looks to the fence and at a point opposite the open rear hatch of the Huron. A group of Zees teeter. They act more riled than their surrounding brethren. In a small group, they part as they bump into each other. Another zomb is revealed laying on the muddy ground.

A young woman.

A statuesque blond in her better days, she looks Amazonian with legs up to her neck. One of those long gams is missing, thus her prone position on the ground. She still shows spirit in her unliving state. She snarls, hisses through cracked black lips. Her rheumy eyes lock on Stokes.

Stokes dips his index and middle finger into the open can, digs out a gooey dollop of the meat byproduct, flings it at the tattered woman. Some of the red puree hits her, some splatters on the ground near her. She sluggishly gropes for the stuff. Her undead brothers and sisters step over her, step on her, snatch up the scraps before she can. A large dab lands on her hip and is raked up, along with a chunk of her diseased flesh, the diner caring little for what he munches on.

"You don't have anything better to do?" Billet says with a furrowed brow, the raindrops pour off like a small waterfall.

Stokes glances up at the gray gloom above, chews the butt of his stogy like a rabbit with a carrot, then looks down at Billet. "As a matter of fact, sir... I do not."

"Well, quit abusing that poor girl and do something constructive."

"She started it."

Jake huffs in exasperation, blows out the frustration and expletives he wants to heap on the man. "When she was on *this side* of the dirt," he, instead, replies, knowing the kind of women Stokes liked and how he treated them. Agitation fades. *She probably kicked his balls into his throat one night and he's never gotten over it.*

"Hey, Captain Hero, trouble with your misfits?"

Billet's shoulders bunch as the voice, followed by the man, step around the front of his rig. Jeremy Pike, commander of the Devastator—the Abrams tank sitting further down the line—steps up wearing a grin, exudes his usual pomposity.

Billet looks the other way so the man can't see his irritated sneer and replies: "I was wondering when you'd meander down this way." He turns to the TC with regained composure. "Tired of sitting in your comfy little iron coffin?"

"I could ask the same," Pike says. He shirks the raindrops off his olive drab poncho. The rain jacket hands from his large frame, an oversized man in an undersized tent. "I'm sure you're wandering the line soaking up more praise?"

Shoulders slump. "Here we go…" Jake groans.

Pike continues: "I hear little else these days except the success of your mission and how you brought the big NSC commissioner to justice last September. Hell, I'm surprised I didn't roll into town last month to find Grand Rapids renamed Billetville."

Seven months since. Jesus Christ. Billet clenches a fist, arm tense, muscles coil. His face grows red, though not entirely with anger. "What brings you down, Major? I'm sure it's not just to give me the berries."

Pike places his ham hock fists to his sides and peers up and down the line like a king surveying his serfs.

"Just checking the morale of the men."

Billet snorts. *Rii-ight.*

It had been the second time he'd seen the man walk the line since stationed here. Pike spent more time in his tank or making quick trips back across to the city for who knew what.

"Besides, I think my men are going to mutiny if I win another game of Poker."

"Well, thanks for coming out where the real action is." Billet glances out at the undead citizenry wandering along the fence line.

Currently—and thankfully—there is nothing going on. Other than the little scene Stokes stirred, the Zees aren't doing much more than bumping into each other; packed in and piled up.

You can't find your way back through the Pearl Street underpass, Billet looks at the undead, *can't get back to your main hood, out of the rain, away from the city.*

The storm has driven what seems the whole of the UCRA folk east, back towards the downtown area. They are small children rushing to the comfort of their parents as the sky crashes and lightning strobes. The walking dead don't want to leave the close proximity to their living relatives and friends, the living folk who stay behind secured bridges and barricades protecting downtown Grand Rapids.

Billet looks back at Pike, finds the man thumbing the trackball of a small handheld device. Jake's seen the devices before. He's surprised Pike's obtained one, and is being so obvious about it.

"I didn't know you partake of such things," Billet says, leans forward enough to see the small four inch color screen. It shows a street schematic of their current location. Several colored dots blink in the general vicinity, though on the other side of the enclosure. Jake estimates there are about a dozen dots on the screen. "If any of those carry bourbon, point them out."

Pike curls his lip, looks down his nose at Billet. Wiping the rain drops from the device's face, he turns it so Jake can no longer spy the screen.

"If they carried alcohol that would be much more preferable I am certain." Pike says looking at the handheld.

"Green: marijuana. Orange: LSD. White: cocaine. You can't kick the dealers for tryin'." Stokes hangs over the side of the Huron like a vulture above Pike's head. "Though I'm not one to corral a rotter and dig in its guts for a bag of dope."

Pike looks up, anger and annoyance on his face.

"You dealing or buying?" Stokes says, grinning ear to ear, and follows with a tone of false innocence. "I've never seen a purple dot before. What's that type carrying?"

Pike snarls, turns the handheld, and tilts it back in Billet's direction. Jake sees the blinking purple dot, the only one in the small crowd of its more colorful companions. He knows what the handheld signifies.

Pike slaps the device against his wet rain slicker before Billet can pinpoint where the dot is located within the crowd of Zees opposite them.

It's close.

The Major looks up at the amused gunner again, daggers in

his eyes. "Keep it up, soldier. There's lots of room in the brig."

Stokes' humor blows out like an overloaded electrical transformer. "The brig is under water." The new GRCC barracks and command center is nestled across the river, downtown in the Grand Plaza Hotel, its basement and lower detention facility flooded.

It is Pike's turn to grin. "Exactly. How long can you hold your breath, Sergeant?"

"That's enough." Billet breaks in. "Sergeant, Phelps might need a break from going over things with our new navigator. Grab him and get an inventory of our Z-rations so I can report out to Major Pike.

"And tell Eddie to come top side. If he isn't done cleaning the Head…"

"I'm here, Captain." Specialist Edward "Eddie" Mulholland responds in a thick southern drawl. He rises from the front left cupola of the HTV like a periscope, just as tall and thin.

"Rear gun detail."

"As usual, sir-rah." Mulholland salutes, not once looking Billet in the eye. The lanky gunner down periscopes, disappears into the bowels of the transport, and pops up like a gopher in one of Huron's rear rooftop hatchways.

Pike watches the whole thing, brushes several rivulets of rainwater from the brim of his hood. "Other than being out of his element up here with us Yanks, does the boy have a problem with his superiors?"

Billet tries not to think on it. "No. If the kid and Stokes were up for commendation, Stokes would help him haul his wheelbarrow full."

Pike smirks. "I don't see the hero worship in that grunt like so many of the others bestow upon you."

The tank commander is an expert knife fighter, something Jake learned back when they'd gone through Basic together. Billet still wears a scar across his left breast from a bout with the man. *Seems a life time ago,* he thinks.

Pike can still cut without pulling the big combat knife Jake knows he carries beneath the rain poncho. Billet can tell Pike notices something about his crew, something that crawls and festers just below the surface. And Pike can obviously see it in the face and hear it in the response from Mulholland.

It stabs the heart, the pride, and cuts deep. Jake knows he compromised his leadership and the respect from his crew seven months ago since the Lettner mission. He went off the deep end; let his stern military professionalism slough away at missions end as they brought William Lettner—the late NSC commissioner—home. Jake still feels the burn at letting his anger boil away rationale. He recalls the lakeshore regent getting the best of him at missions end, more words than actions. He shot the unarmed man even as Lettner was cuffed and in the custody of his peers. His crew has not looked at him the same since.

He is no hero. No fucking hero at all.

Suddenly tired, Billet looks at the handheld Pike holds. He changes the subject. "What's with the tracking app? You aren't going buggy on us, are you?"

Pike's gaze falls upon the blinking screen. Billet can tell the strange purple dot is the Major's focus.

"As if you should talk," the big tank commander says, tries to twist the psychological blade he also wields deep into Jake's gut. "Not at all, Captain, not at all.

"I've been tasked this time by our superiors," Pike says matter-of-factly. "Seems the discontinued vaccine the government was so happy to bestow upon us first responders during the outbreak is now being sold on the black market by dealers of other illicit drugs."

Billet's brows rise. He's heard rumors, but...

"I know life sucks nowadays. People look more for altered states of mind to escape." The TC inhales deep, his broad chest billows. He exhales slowly. "But alter the body to try to escape into some realm of supposed immortality? You'd think the daily view of the unliving multitudes would make people think otherwise about subjecting their physical shells to such damnation."

A mental image of Rebecca Regan enters Jake's mind from last September while in Reganshire, with Lettner hidden in Huron's bowels. Her bandaged arms wept bloody fluids, and her skin gray as ash. He knew the woman was doing something to herself but he had suspected she was simply supping off the black blood of captured ZT's—zombie troopers. It only made sense now, her and Old Man Regan illegally acquiring the same shit the military had been given to fight the contagion years ago.

"So what's the city council and high command bequeathed you?" Billet asks, eyes locked on the handheld Pike retains in a death grip close to his chest.

The TC's eyes shoot left and right, and then he leans close. "I've been tasked to track any Zee who is carrying pure Datropoline, and…"

He suddenly stiffens and goes tight-lipped. His brow furrows, dark gaze locked on Billet. "I'm…not supposed to talk about it. It's a covert op…" Pike says, resumes his usual haughtiness, "…like yours was."

Jake tightens his jaw to keep from vomiting a mass of obscenities upon his "superior." It is childish, fucking petty, how Pike regards him. They'd followed each other up the military food chain. Jeremy always struggled; all his hot-aired bravado chapped people's ass, and usually his own. When the TC made Major, it had been rubbed in Billet's face.

And it still burned Pike's ass Jake had been chosen to take the Lettner mission.

Don't test your luck now, Jacob, Jake thinks. *Keep your job. Don't go swimming in the brig for insubordination.*

He focuses on the steady staccato of the cold droplets upon

his head: "If you need any assistance, Major." Billet says with a salute.

The Huron's new navigator appears at rooftop via Stokes's hatch. The 24-year old soldier is the same age as Billet's son would have been this year. The young man racks his head on the hard composite grips of Stokes's mounted quad .30's. He grimaces, rubs the crown of his bruised skull case. The kid clears his throat, face growing red, as he sees Billet and the Major look at him. He adjusts the faded Chicago SOX cap covering his shaved head and returns their gaze.

"Captain, I got a call from Command on a priority channel for ya." Specialist Colter Campau says. He salutes the Major as the big man makes eye contact.

Billet hears a low growl from Pike and expects to see the rain hiss off his anger-hot skin. He cannot look at him without a grin, so instead, casts his gaze towards the enclosure.

The neighborhood Zees press against the tall chain link fence, washed yb the steady downpour but look no cleaner for it. They amass near Billet and Pike's location, drawn as if attracted by Pike and his aggressive kinship.

Jake notices one particular Zee standing by its lone self. It faces forward, stares back directly at him. While the other unliving denizens continue to move about, shuffling around the male Zee, this one stands stock still. The dead fellow with the mottled black hair, a chunk of scalp hanging red and loose from the right side of its head, seems especially interested in him.

"What the fuck?" Jake folds his arms across his chest. He holds himself, fighting a shiver of uneasiness with the creature staring at him.

The living dead man folds arms across its sunken chest, like a fucked up mirror image.

"Captain?" The young navigator says.

Billet looks up at Campau, and only for a second back towards the peculiar Zee.

It's gone.

Billet shakes his head. *Out in the field too long,* he thinks.

Jake starts to pull himself up the rungs to the Huron's rooftop. He feels a hard tug at his wet pant leg.

"You tell me what's going on, Captain. You come tell me on the double, you got that?" Pike snarls, as the sky rumbles above, growling in agreement. He lets go of Billet's leg and stomps back through the slop towards his own vehicle.

Billet shakes his head, clambers to the slippery rooftop of the Huron.

One high step to the Huron's top side, Billet hears the snickers of Stokes from below Campau.

"Aw, jeezuz," Jake groans, shaking his head. "There's no call from Command, is there?"

"No, sir." Campau responds straight faced, a little red.

"Stokes put you up to this?"

Somewhere off in the distance, northward, a high pitched whine can be heard.

"No, sir," Campau says. "It was my idea, sir. You seemed in trouble, sir, so…"

At the rear gunner's turret, Mulholland looks ready to duck and cover.

Billet balances against the side of the transport and slides his beret from his head. He rolls it between his fists, squeezes out the soaked material. He places it back on his head.

Stokes quits chuckling.

The overhead whine grows louder, barely discernible over the downpour and the lamentation of the nearby zombs.

Jake looks down at the olive-colored camo pattern of the Huron. He can't help but smirk. He looks up at his new crew member. "You'll fit in fine."

The whine grows louder, turns into a rapid gurgling buzz as it draws closer. It separates into two distinct sounds.

Billet squints through the gray sheet of rain. Two small aircraft head towards them, dropping in from the north, straight toward the riverbank command.

The troops along the perimeter of the enclosure start to move about. They arm up their weapons; bright orange ammo clips stand out under the shroud of the dim day.

"Aircraft incoming. Nine o'clock and eleven." Billet says, stealing a glance at Mulholland.

Odd thing. In this instance perhaps not a good thing, the city nor the GRCC possess airplanes.

Chapter Two
Crushed to Dead

"**I**s this a joke?" Jake growls.

Stokes pops up, assumes his front turret position as Campau goes below. "They aren't drones," the gunner says flatly.

Billet watches the two small planes drop from the sky. Initially hard to discern their size against the downpour, they close in on the riverfront assembly. He sees they are not full-sized aircraft. They are not UAVs.

As the two planes buzz their way earthward Jake sees they are radio-controlled hobby aircraft. A mock-up of an A-10 Warthog flies several feet and below a gull-winged F4U Corsair model.

"Where'd they come from?" Jake asks as the Corsair pulls ahead of the other plane. It angles up sharply, nose towards the heavens as if it's going to try to reach for the low hanging clouds.

Mulholland snaps up a pair of binoculars. He brings them to his eyes, lowers them, wipes his eyes, then the lenses and raises them again. He tries to focus in on the edge of the downtown river bank.

The radio-controlled A-10 tries to follow the Corsair. It climbs, drops, sputters, drops, and goes to climbs again. Its small gas engine burps. The plane drops, heading closer and closer to the ground. With one last burst, it angles up, then downward, barrel rolls as it dives to the earth.

"Shee-it," Billet swears as the plane drops behind the enclosure and spears into the midst of the undead.

A horrible wail erupts from the Zees. They move in unison and push against the fence. The front row mashes their rotting faces against the chain link. Trapped, they cannot move forward as the second and third wave of spooked Zees press against them. Immobile with hundreds of pounds behind them, the front unliving folk respond.

Decomposed flesh, rotted organs and weak bones break and pop.

Mangled faces and upper bodies balloon against the fencing, burst and ooze through the chain link like sausage through a meat grinder.

An orange-yellow glow erupts where the r/c aircraft went down.

Billet clambers to the Huron's rooftop to see what's burning. "Ah, double shit," he says as he finds his answer.

Flames consume a hapless male Zee. He wobbles unsteadily with the cockpit and fuselage of the A-10 through his soft gut. The small amount of fuel the plane has dispensed ignites, turning the fellow into a torch. He stops, stands in place, head angled down, looking at himself as he is consumed.

Flesh and fat sizzle, pop.

Like hungry picnickers to a grill, his fellows surge towards him. The rain and wet clothing keep them from being set ablaze. They crowd against their flaming comrade, snuffing him like a candle.

Melted flesh leaves the cooked Zee gummy. Red-black tendrils trail off of him, adhering to his companions as they back away.

The Corsair continues its skyward swoop. It spirals, then sputters, as the wet takes its toll. With a final cough, it drops, earthbound. Its shrill engine screams its own horror filled cry. It makes the living wince as it dives towards the mix of undead civilians.

Stokes opens fire with his quad .30's, makes Billet's heart skip a beat as rubber-tipped bullets fly skyward. Jake grits his teeth, glares at Stokes as the gunner lets his fingers off the triggers.

"What?" Stokes says, acts like a kid with a hand caught in the cookie jar.

The radio-controlled Corsair doesn't need Stokes assistance. It levels out last second, and screams over the undead and the living. It misses the fence top by inches as it rushes by. Its wings dip left, right, whoever controls it trying to correct its flight path. With one last short spiral climb, it flips, and dives nose first into the churning waters of the Grand River.

If the controller's intention of the wayward aircrafts is to bring the already-simmering zombie populace to a boil, it burst the cooking pot as well. The plane's flight path works like a sheep dog directing its flock, the undead throng push even harder towards the river and against the already strained enclosure.

It is the soggy GRCC's turn to wail in protest as two spans of the enclosure bulge outward, buckle, and collapse against the weight of the surging Zees. Foot soldiers unable to get out of the way go down with it. They slap to the sodden ground, the loosened metal links rattle and ring like tiny dinner bells. One fence section sags and falls against the rear of the Huron, possibly a godsend as it keeps another from crumpling.

"Get those men out of there!" Billet yells as the grunts who avoid the toppled fence start to back away from the oncoming dead.

A few soldiers panic. Weapons rise. They start firing into the advancing mob.

The west side civilians lurch forward. They are panicked by the storm, by the airborne assault, by the shouting soldiers and gun fire. They sense the downed fence, an opening for escape from the frenzied locale. They claw and climb over each other, push, punch, and maul to get beyond the fence line.

"What's happening over there?" Pike's voice crackles in Billet's earbud.

Stokes hangs over Huron's side, offers a hand to fellow soldiers rushing to climb to the vehicle's rooftop, away from the chaos on the ground.

Mulholland switches rear guns to the side where the fencing has fallen, aims but doesn't fire.

"We've got a breech in the enclosure. Our neighbors are coming into our yard. Fire! Fire! Drive them back!" Billet replies, adjusting his throat mic.

A sudden burst of firearms drowns out the rumbling sky.

Mulholland fires quick short bursts at the ground and lower extremities. He avoids upper body and head shots as even hard-punching rubber bullets will shred a Zee. All the Gurks fire low, knee-cap if possible; avoid soft craniums. They all know the laws relating to the neighboring dead civvies.

"Don't let them beyond the enclosure." Pike orders.

Warning sirens blare within the city. Through the rain haze, Billet makes out movement of the big emergency gates: solid steel apertures which run the length of the street on the opposite city-side of the bridge. They slowly draw closed, cutting off the heavily-populated downtown area to the outside world.

Jake sees the Devastator buttoned up tight while Pike gives orders from within. The 120mm cannon faces the west while the rest of the vehicle swivels around, churning the sodden grass into mud. The .50-caliber machine gun at the Commander's Weapon Station stands quiet as does the M240 machine gun in front of the loader's hatch, and the second M240 to the right of the cannon. Pike and crew aren't coming out unless they have to, but the guns are positioned to divert any undead visitors if they try to get to the Pearl Street Bridge.

"That's right," Jake says as the city gates shut tight. "Leave us out here like unwanted scrap."

A trooper doesn't see a Zee limp towards his flank as he fires at the oncoming throng. The creature opens its black maw and raises its arm to strike.

Billet pulls his pistol and fires.

The orange-tip round slaps the Zee in the shoulder, throws it sideways, it topples, hits the ground. It struggles to push itself up on hands and knees. The creature's sluggishness gives the trooper time to raise his rifle and rap it in the head, solid, hard enough to daze and steal consciousness. The zomb goes down in the mud, doesn't rise. The trooper moves on to fight the next undead citizen.

"We're coming to assist." The TC of the M60 tank says.

Billet sees the man before he hears him. Tall, lanky fellow, reminds him of Mulholland. Donovan, Sergeant. Jake doesn't know him very well other than he's Canadian and came from the Detroit area.

"What're you doing, Sergeant?" Pike says over the comm.

"Helping."

"Get back to your vehicle, Sergeant."

"Negative, sir. We're out to help. There're too many civilians roaming the grounds anyway. If we accidentally steamroll one, or a dozen, are you paying my fine?" Donovan challenges Pike.

No response.

Billet grins.

"I'll man up when we can roll again." Donovan says and nods up at Billet as he and two of his crew run by. The third crewman stays at the M60's commander's hatch, hands on the .50-Cal.

The Gurks fire at feet, fire into the air. They whistle and yell like cowboys at a cattle drive as they slowly turn back the escaping civilians. The unliving who keep advancing are knocked down and subdued without further injury. Some clamber back over the enclosure, they try to climb fence, try to climb each other. They fall, roll, rake, snarl.

It is a scene of pure chaos, Billet thinks, and sadly comical.

The civilians who thrust back towards the enclosure, scratch, claw and bite at others who still try to exit.

"Keep pushing them back," Billet yells as he slides off the front end of the Huron. He lands, unbalanced in the mid, almost goes down on his face. He regains his footing and plants boots firmly in the brown slop. He fires at the feet of Zees, some with shoes, others bare foot; all gray, rotting flesh. He fires until his orange clip is spent.

A soldier stumbles backwards against Huron's slick side and goes down. He grimaces, drops his assault rifle in his lap. His nose leans against his cheek, broken. Blood runs down his face.

"They kick like mules," the soldier says out the side of his mouth. His eyes roll as he fights to keep conscious.

"Medic!" Jake squats beside him. "You'll be fine." He takes up the assault rifle. "I'll return this to you."

A soldier—red cross on his helmet—slips toward them through the mud. Jake stands, waves, points down at the Gurk at his feet.

Stokes lands beside Jake, feet fumble, try to gain traction in the slippery brown slop. He grabs Jake's arm for support, nearly putting Jake on his ass. The sergeant pulls his sidearm as he rises. Gritting his tobacco-stained teeth, the gunner shoots a Zee that rakes at a female trooper.

The undead civilian's head snaps back but does not return upright. It vanishes, its neck a sludgy fount of black blood and brain matter.

Jake glances at the clip of Stokes's pistol. No orange designation. Full metal jacket.

"Gawddammit, Stokes!"

"It's the only way to meet chicks nowadays." Stokes nods and smiles at the female Gurk.

She looks at her savior, her face runny with rain and blood from the head shot.

Billet cannot tell if she is grateful or annoyed being gore-washed via his crewman's assistance.

He tears the pistol from Stokes' hand, replaces it with the procured rifle. He envisions fines, docked pay, potential court hearings. Blowing the head off a city dweller's undead relative, even during a fight for survival, equals a whole lot of trouble.

A new UCRA citizen steps behind the female Gurk: a giant male Zee in a muddy, tattered plaid shirt and wet khaki dress slacks. She registers the brute's presence a breath before black finger nails rake across her throat. She falls, grips her slender neck, blood gushing between her fingers.

"Get her out of here," Jake yells. A nearby trooper jumps to action.

The soldier grabs his colleague, begins to drag her away. The monster steps forward, swings a meaty fist. It clocks the man in the head, almost topples him and his dying companion.

The big Zee growls like a bear as a barrage of rubber brutality drives him back.

"Status?" Pike bellows over the comm.

Come out of your fucking hole and find out, Billet wants to respond. "We're turning them back, but have some stubborn residents." He watches the big male push forward. It shrugs the rubber rounds off like they are throwing annoying pebbles at it.

A few bewildered but ardent fellow rotters follow the giant.

A body builder, or simply a guy in damn good shape before the virus fucked him into unlife, the rhino of a man swats and claws his way through the line of soldiers. Rubber munitions continue to pelt him. His followers—two sexless, gore-weeping abominations, and a smaller male and female who stay close together—trudge, totter and fight behind the big fellow.

"Captain, permission to move the rig to block the exit,"

Huron's driver, Lance Corporal Loutonia Phelps comes over the comm.

The HTV's twin diesels roar to life, then are lost in the gun fire below and thunder from above.

"No. We're snagged on the fence," the voice of Campau cuts in.

The bark of Mulholland's rear gun informs Jake the location of their new navigator.

The huge Zee—the Rhino, Billet decides—sweeps aside a pair of Gurks as it draws closer to the swollen river.

"If we pull out," Campau adds, "we'll bring further sections of the enclosure down."

A Zee stumbles within arm's reach of Billet. He cracks it in the skull. It drops to its hands and knees in homage to him. It tries to rise, snarling. Stokes stills it with a heavy blow from his rifle butt.

"Any ideas?" Billet says to Campau.

"Back us up."

Phelps comes online. "You talking to me or the Captain?"

"Uh, you, ma'am."

Rhino drops out of sight below a brushy berm which hugs the edge of the swollen river. His group of four follow close behind.

"You got civilians about to slip into the river." Pike breaks in, pissed, frantic. "Don't let it make the river."

How in the hell? Billet wonders how Pike knows sitting within the bowels of the Devastator. It takes a second for the cogs to turn. Then: *His handheld tracking device.*

The Huron's engines huff as the vehicle throttles up.

"Reversing, Captain." Loutonia says.

"*Captain...*" Pike again. Loud. Angry. Nearly bursts Jake's eardrums.

Billet looks to the soldiers at the river bank. There are a dozen of them. He can't see Rhino's followers but the big Zee is back up at the berm's crest. A trooper moves behind it, to bar its retreat to the river. The brute swings, connects with a blow so savage it snaps the poor Gurk's head almost 180 degrees.

Jake knows the grunt is dead before he goes ragdoll.

The Rhino turns and stumbles with heavy feet back down the berm.

"They're going in," a soldier calls. "They've all gone into the river."

"Dammit," Billet moans, picturing five walking corpses dropping in the drink, wet logs that bob through the churning waters before they're swallowed by the swollen river.

Huron's engines roar. The big rig starts to back up.

Pike's Abrams barks to life as well.

"Get out of the way. I'll take care of this," Pike yells in everyone's earbud.

The Huron jerks rearward.

In his rear gunner's position, Mulholland hangs on, watches the corner of the transport. The curly concertina wire looms so close he could touch it.

Loutonia gives the Huron a touch more gas.

The massive transport vehicle lurches.

Lying at a 45 degree angle, the fence line jumps, rattles, and starts to rise from its leaning position.

The Abrams snarls towards them, moves fast—too fast— across the crowded and narrow ground.

Stokes swears loudly, tackles two grunts that aren't paying attention. They roll in a mass of tangled limbs through the mud. The 68-ton tank grinds over the spot where they had just stood.

"Move over," Pike says as the Abrams sidles close to the front end of the Huron. The tank's driver's side hard rubber track nudges the lower cowl of the armored transport.

"Oh, no, you didn't just do that," Loutonia's angry voice over the airwaves.

Proud of her maintenance of the Huron, Jake is glad she

doesn't expound more than that on the Devastator's light kiss to their rig.

"Major, you dialing it in a little close," Jake says as he watches the Huron jump backwards, Loutonia trying to avoid further contact with Pike's vehicle.

Mulholland goes sideways against his hatch coaming. His earbud pops out, dangles by its wire at his shoulder.

The leaning fence segment snaps perfectly upright. It causes the downed section to regain some angle and height. The UCRA citizens who climb over or lay atop it are flung backwards. They pile in a heap on their own side of the enclosure.

"Get some Z-rations over there," Billet calls out as he watches three muddy grunts put the beat down on one last shambler still standing on their side of the enclosure. They empty their frustration on the thing. *I hope no one sees that from across the river.* Jake shakes his head.

Pike's turret hatch opens with a squeal and the tank commander props himself up through the aperture.

"Gawddamnit! What did I say about letting them get too close to the river?" he snaps at the tired, wet grunts. "We gotta account for every single gawddamn one of those civilians."

Stokes slogs up beside Billet. "What crawled up his ass?"

"Not what crawled, but *who* is going to crawl up his ass when we go back across the river." Billet wipes a trickle of rain water from his brow. Lights in building across the river glare, a multitude of eyes upon them. He can see faces in those windows. *Shit.*

Jake walks to the berm. The muddy ground pulls at his boots. Rhino and his lackeys are nowhere to be seen, swept downstream in the deluge. Somebody's non-living friends have gone MIA on the GRCC's watch. It means a definite ass chewing by the city council, and the friends and relatives of the lost.

"Captain, sir, down here." A Gurk waves, directs Billet back to the spot where the enclosure had collapsed.

Several soldiers had not been able to escape the fence when it toppled. While a handful of troops dragged the beaten undead folk to a secure point surrounded by other armed soldiers, another half dozen Gurks pluck their torn battle brothers and sisters from the grassy mire where the fence had fallen.

"Excuse us, sir." Two soldiers carry an unconscious grunt between them. The wounded's military greens dark with blood. The man must have been pinned sidelong when the fence came down. His entire right side, from head to hip, is poked, torn and gored; the spot his friends had taken him from a blend of brown mixed with dark crimson.

Billet steps aside to let them pass as he moves towards the trooper who summons him.

"Captain." A small, pain-filled voice calls to Jake.

A soaked soldier with a long, weeping gash across the side of his face kneels before another soldier who's been literally crushed into the sodden earth.

"Dammit," Billet growls as he goes down on a knee beside the other soldier and the grunt pressed into the bloody mire. "I'll take it from here. Go get taken care of," he says to the wounded Gurk who stands vigil over the downed man.

The soldier climbs unsteadily to his feet, salutes Jake weakly and limps away.

"Captain," the small voice says again at Billet's mucky boots.

"Quiet, son." Jake reaches down and clasps Wills hand. He glances over his shoulder, waves to a medic who treats another soldier.

Wills appears to have been run face-first up and down a massive cheese grater. The impression of the chain link fence still shows on his wet skin and clothing. His uniform: shredded to strips. Exposed flesh: raked away by sharp broken finger nails of undead citizens he'd been sworn to protect. Internal organs push through his open side.

Face a bloody smear, Wills nose has been bitten clean off. His cheeks are serrated flaps. Blood pools in the torn pulp of his right eye. In shock, the mortally wounded soldier's system refuses to let him drift off into the painless black ether of unconsciousness.

"Don't... let them take me... to Butterworth," Wills says in a tiny voice, bloody froth at his lips. "I don't want to be a ZT."

He fears being taken to the test facility where they make a semi-undead creature out of a mortally wounded soldier. It is done by morbid science and man's insane scheming.

"Don't worry, kid," Jake says. *Lucky you. You head for game's end.*

Now banned, in the early days of the virus and zombie affliction, Datropoline vaccines were given to every soldier who signed on to fight and protect.

"As long as your head remains attached," Jake remembers his first CO's words, "all is well and dandy. Beyond that, if you take a bad one for the team, the Dat has a nasty side effect."

Jake still gets the chills thinking on it. His commander's words: "It doesn't let you die."

Die, but not in a dead-dead, not separated from one's mortal coil, not see Saint Peter-dead. If brain and heart still fire, and military skill and training remain...

"Sew an arm of someone less fortunate. Re-attach a leg. Stitch a gaping gut hole. Clip ya. Chip ya for radio-controlled mayhem," more words from the old CO, *"then you're a goddamn ball buster again, ready for another go at the front line. Hoo-ah!"*

And in West Michigan, if a grunt fell with fatal wounds, off to the Butterworth Test Facility they'd go for all the fixin's.

Bureaucrats still did the darnedest things.

It played hell with one's head. No GI wants to be in an in-between state of living and unliving, and a somewhat semi-controlled killing automaton for the government or city they work for.

"We have more coming over the fence," someone says over the

comm.

The re–propped fence is a three feet away. Bloody faces snarl and hiss. Jake looks up to find some of the rotting west siders climb atop their brethren to make their way back over. The first few snag in the concertina wire. They create padding for the others to climb over.

Pike snarls something loud and colorful over the comm, and suddenly the big Abrams growls forward a few more feet. It stops, parallel to the weakened section of fencing. The 120mm gun swivels round until it faces westward towards the UCRA neighborhood.

Don't do it! Billet raises hands to cover ears as the tank cannon angles up a breath.

The Devastator's right track spins while the left stands locked. The Abrams turns itself in the same direction as its cannon.

Billet glances up to see a dozen civilians ready to drop on top of him.

Jake winces as Pike's .50-Cal lights up as does the tank's M240s. He isn't sure if Pike and crew fire rubber rounds but the undead civvies fall back in an eruption of bullet-chewed meaty bits.

He leans over the young soldier to shield him from the flesh shrapnel. "Hang in there, kid. I won't let you go. We'll get you to the city hospital and…"

Unblinking, Private Wills one good eye stares far beyond anything earthly. Rain drops hit the faded pupil, pool, and then run in small rivulets, like a tear, down the side of the soldiers face.

"Dammit," Billet growls.

The poor grunt is done but not out of the game. If the medical yahoos at the test facility can get their hands on the body within twenty-four hours they get themselves a fresh walking soldier corpse.

He has given his word to the kid.

With Stoke's sidearm in hand, live rounds in the clip, Jake puts the gun to Wills' forehead. Hot lead deliverance and no prolonged torment.

Billet wraps his finger round the trigger.

Overhead, the sound of helicopter blades breaks his concentration.

One of the city's helicopters slashes through the gloom, flies over the river and the drenched troops and vehicles. Beneath it, a huge crate swings. The old Apache gunship clears the enclosure fence line; the ropes about the crate fall away. The container drops, nose dives into the ground, and cracks open like a huge wooden egg.

In a slow but steady stream, the UCRA civilians who are so eager to come eastward, turn and head towards the smashed crate. They attack it with ferocious vigor, the contents: hundreds of pounds of Z-rations.

A hand clamps onto Jake's shoulder. He jerks, almost pulls the trigger.

"Can I help you, Captain?" A grunt asks, a red cross on his helmet. Behind him, Jake sees other medics rush in with a line of new soldiers.

The tall steel gates across the bridge discharge a fresh batch of troops. Flashing lights and the growl of other heavy vehicles come from behind the men, waiting as the slowly re-opening aperture grinds wide enough to allow them egress.

Reinforcements! Hoo-ah! But too late for a handful of service men and women who lay about the muddy, bloody ground.

Jake eases the sidearm under his jacket and turns to the medic. He catches a look from Mulholland atop the Huron, the gunner's eyes transfixed on his jacket covered hand.

Eddie looks away, a harried expression on his gaunt face.

"This soldier is *not* to be brought to the BTF," Billet says to the medic who kneels beside the body of Private Wills. "Do you understand..." Jake looks at the medical soldiers name tape on the right breast pocket of his ACU. "...do you understand, Corporal Hampton?"

Checks Wills to make sure the man's dead. "Yes, sir, but you know it is not up to m…"

"I will hold you personally responsible if I see this man upright and back out in the field." Jake opens his jacket enough for the medic to see the pistol.

The medic's eyes narrow. He closes Wills one open eye and puts the soldier's hands gently at his sides. "No disrespect, Captain… Billet," pulls the same routine on Jake, putting *his* name to memory, "Are you threatening me?"

Strength and anger rush away like water down an open manhole. "I'm sorry," Billet replies, "Please, see that this man gets a proper burial and, not used…again."

"I'll do what I can do, sir, but he signed on like we all did. The protocol is…"

Billet turns away before he does or says anything more damning.

Protocol. If the city council had their way, the GRCC would all be a "dead" puppet army fighting for them—puppets with no will of their own. Mayor Honeywell doesn't lean that way, but there are others, Jake knows. There are folks within the city with hearts more rotten and foul than UCRA civilians.

He shakes his head and chastises himself for his thoughts. Voicing opinions, even letting thoughts fester like that are not good. They are not good for a man in his position, let alone his career.

Heavy with mud, Billet's boots are lead weights. He is tired. *That's what it is*, he tells himself.

"Captain." Stokes meets him at the rungs to the transport as a group of fresh troops skirt around the Huron in a hurry.

The soldiers carry steel struts in hand to further prop and secure the fence line closer to original position.

"Thought you were going to shoot the guy," Stokes says with a slight chuckle. He can see Jake is not in a good mood.

"Which one?" Jake pulls Stokes' sidearm from the folds of his jacket. "If I find you disobeying orders again," he warns, refers to the live rounds in the gun, "it might be you." He brusquely shoves the pistol into Stokes' hands.

James Stokes opens his mouth to reply, but closes it without uttering a word. He glances up to see Mulholland watching, the rear gunner's despondent look reveals he has witnessed the short exchange.

Catching Stokes eyeing him, Eddie Mulholland turns his attention to the fence as other soldiers work to shore it up.

Stokes shrugs, holsters the pistol and walks away to assist the other Gurks.

The rungs of the Huron are cold and wet. Billet struggles to the top of the vehicle.

Loutonia appears in the forward gunner's hatch. Her face awash with worry, she offers a Nomex-gloved hand to him. Jake smiles weakly, and lets her strong arm pull him the rest of the way up.

"Are you hurt?" she asks as his knees make the steel roofline.

He turns, plops down on his rear on the wet rooftop of the HTV.

"Fine. Just… tired."

Head slumps. His arms feel like I-beams. He pulls the beret from his head, feebly wrings the moisture out. No further droplets fall from the heavens. The rains cease, short lived as he knows it will be. Dark gray clouds drift low overhead, a rumble of thunder quakes in the distance, more to come.

Loutonia puts a hand on his shoulder, gives it a gentle squeeze, concerned.

"I'm fine. Really," Jake says. Lying. *I feel like shit.*

"Captain Billet," Pike's voice rings across the span between the Huron and the Devastator.

Jake slowly raises his head.

"Got a call from Central." Hesitation. "*I* did." Pike says proudly. "We're supposed to get into town pronto. Follow me in."

"Roger that… sir." Jake gives him a half-ass salute, not out to insult, just out of steam.

Pike sneers at him.

Men scatter as the Abrams revs, does a 180 and tracks tear a muddy furrow in the wet soil.

"Button it up, gang. We're Oscar Mike." Billet says. He checks the progress of the engineers ratcheting a third bracing pole against the fence.

The line stands tall again.

Stokes clambers aboard as Loutonia drops back down inside the carrier. A few heart beats and the twin diesels throttle up.

On hands and knees, Jake moves to the command hatch. He looks to Mulholland but the kid has already moved down below.

Been a bitch of a time for everyone, Billet thinks as he slips into the dark hole of his command hatch. *The kid's being evasive about something though.*

Checking one last time to verify everything is secure topside, Billet gives a half-hearted wave to Donovan, the M60's TC.

Already heading across the bridge, the Devastator is passed by the three remaining M6 Bradley Linebackers the GRCC has in its arsenal of combat vehicles. Additional Gurks and another BRV-O follow them.

A fresh rain drop hits Jake's face. The sky rumbles. He groans.

He gives the towering buildings across the swollen river a wary glance before he ducks inside and closes the hatch.

Billet knows the storm is going to be bigger on the other side of the river soon.

Losing men and losing UCRA civilians, he has a sinking feeling he is going to be a lightning rod for abuse.

***

A lone male Zee watches the Huron pull away. Its black hair is wet and matted to its head where a flap of loose scalp hangs like the tongue of a bloody shoe. It pays no heed to its rotting brethren who sniff and snarl at the chunks of Z-ration at the lone Zees feet.

Scratching at Black Hair's foot, another male Zee tries to move the appendage so it can get at the meat-slop.

With a surprising burst of speed for an undead being, Black Hair kicks the other in the face. The combat boot it wears obliterates the rotting skull of its fellow like a spoiled melon.

Watching the big HTV drive off, Black Hair turns, pushes aside other Zees intent on the doped grub on the slick ground. He picks up a rucksack lying beside the rusted hulk of an old abandoned car, re-covers the barrel of a Barrett .50 Cal sniper rifle and moves on. He doesn't teeter or shuffle but walks with a normal gait. He heads away from downtown Grand Rapids and goes deeper into the west side neighborhood.

Chapter Three
The Gray Skin of Mourning

"We need your men out there, so you can find the civilians you lost." City Treasurer Rupert Largo says, punctuating the "you" and "yours" with a punch in the gut emphasis. He leans against a polished mahogany table as he addresses the small audience in the meeting room around him.

He scratches at the eye patch covering his right eye. An imposing man in size, he speaks like a military commander versus the main Grand Rapids bean counter. He stands with arms folded across his broad chest. His eye throws daggers at the GRCC lead commander, Colonel Lee Jackson, who sits at the far end of the table.

Behind Largo: the mayor of Grand Rapids, Dennis Honeywell, and a few city council members who have decided to join the lynch mob packed into Mayor Honeywell's office.

Pike and Billet stand at ease behind Jackson. Out of the corner of his eye, Jake sees Pike grit his teeth, surprised the man doesn't open his mouth to respond directly with his usual bravado. The TC doesn't hold back even before the Colonel.

The meeting room is separated by the Mayor's direct office and large administrative work area. Hemmed in west and south by dun-colored walls, the east is one wide, lone picture window that looks out over the city of Grand Rapids. Bulletproof glass separates the meeting room from the admin area. Two score Grand Rapidians pack the room beyond the glass, agitated about the UCRA civilians so close to the city, upset someone's undead relations are floating on a flood raging river heading towards Lake Michigan.

Billet can feel the hot glare from the audience outside the meeting room. The warmth is not comforting.

Colonel Jackson sits calmly while Largo gives him the berries.

"We want you," more emphasis on the *you;* "back out there now, or give your men the orders for a full search and rescue." Largo shakes his index finger at Jackson.

In earlier times, before Jackson had filled the shoes of the prior and late Colonel Renald Neilsen, the blond-haired, thickly muscled and battle-scarred old giant would have launched himself across the table and throttled the life from Largo. Billet wished that would happen. Knowing the sensitivity of the issue, and the folks on the other side of the glass, Jackson understands his place, and takes the razz.

Largo has hammered home his point since the meeting's beginning: the GRCC has inadvertently lost citizen Zees when the barricade went down. The Treasurer has re-iterated it three times now, more to suck up to the mayor, his brother-in-law, than anything. Jackson despises the man, Largo talks too much, pounds his chest like a gorilla.

"Are you prepared to do this? It needs to be done right now."

Jackson waits until Largo is done posturing, then clears his throat loudly. Everyone in the room diverts their attention to him, tensing, expecting him to go nuclear.

"Even now we're getting reports on the few civilians who went into the river during the conflict," Jackson says, glances at Mayor Honeywell, calm as an eye of a hurricane. "The Wealthy Street Outpost has eyes on them. They'll give us an update when they find a safe means to extract them."

Largo stands unflinching.

The mayor glances up at his brother-in-law, rolls his eyes before returning them to Jackson.

"We've finally got word from Butterworth." Jackson continues. "Their communications are up though the place is surrounded by water. That southwest quadrant is flooded quite extensively."

Honeywell nods, perhaps the only one in the room who appreciates the information.

Largo catches the gesture and won't let it lie. "The Intel I have states our civilians you lost have already passed the Wealthy Street Outpost, and we're waiting on permission from Wyoming-Grandville to enter their territory to pursue. You know the drill, Colonel. Citizens wander out of the Neighborhood or go into the river, the nets are deployed."

Billet notices Jackson take a calming breath.

"The storm garbled transmissions." Flames crackle behind those words, but the Colonel keeps it subdued. "Hell, we can't even get reinforcements out there due to all the static. So much for that new comms system you promised us. You lost some Zees. I've dead troopers and some seriously injured men who would've worn better if I could've gotten more of medical teams out there when shit hit the fan."

Images of Wills groping at his feet flash in Jake's mind. He purses his lips, bites his tongue lest he add to the Colonel's statement. He fears he would not be so verbally restrained.

Red faced and ready to blow, Largo looks to the crowd in the office area. Many of them wave their fists in the air before the mayor's interns who try to take their complaints and keep them from storming the conference room.

"We have irate citizens who want justice and want to know their friends and loved ones are safe." Largo points with a dramatic pump of his arm to the group outside the meeting room, the gesture to get the attention of the people out there, so they can see their city council at work for them. "The GRCC owes its constituents immediate action to resolve the issue."

With furrowed brow and eyes growing dark, Jackson chews his lower lip like a dog gnawing at a bone.

In 2013, the H7N9 bird flu pandemic reared its ugly head. It created what others would call the Blight. Most of the afflicted died and rose. The government stepped in and made sure the living and breathing populace knew they, the government, were still there "for the people." Even when a large number of people rose who had passed before 2013, the Higher Ups made it clear the living populace were the most important focus.

Called in from the start, national, state and local armed forces spread out across the United States, mostly in the larger cities and communities. (In instances this action caused great animosity between the big cities and outlying smaller towns and villages.) As the virus and zombie affliction were brought under control—Jake never recalled a full report on *how*—the military was pressed to stay in service in their respective city bases: another division of law enforcement overseen by local ruling bodies. Depending on the situation and location, the city mayors or state governors were the military's new commander-in-chief.

"We will of course do what's required to rectify the situation." The Colonel takes a deep breath, steadies himself. "Most inland roads and areas I can get a team into are underwater. We'll contact affiliates in Wyoming-Grandville and deploy the catch nets at all accessible river crossings."

Once we get out of this circus, Jake thinks.

He notices the crowd in the main office area has simmered down. They refrain from further fist pumping.

"What the GRCC wants to know is: are the people responsible for that little stunt with the radio-controlled aircraft getting the grill like we are?" Jackson leans forward in his seat, meets Largo eye to eye. "If they hadn't done what they did, neither of us would be in this predicament."

"They will be taken care of." Largo says dryly.

The Mayor clears his throat, sees the anger in the Colonel's eyes at the loose statement.

"Councilman Sutter's son and his friend will be tried for their actions," Mayor Honeywell places a hand on Largo's arm as the man starts to open his mouth. "They're in custody right now. They won't be causing any more fuss. They launched their planes from the top floor of the Grand Plaza Tower. They weren't supposed to be up there."

Leon Sutter sits in the conference room with them. He keeps his gaze on the table, and nervously picks on a nonexistent hangnail.

He's probably been put through the ringer too, Billet surmises. But knowing how things go with city council members and their families, Sutter's boy and his accomplice will simply get a slap on the wrist, or maybe do a few days in lock-up. Maybe.

"I'll take the task to locate the citizens," Pike pipes up.

Everyone turns their head, even the Colonel.

"It was on my watch that this tragedy happened. I feel it's my responsibility to clean up my own mess."

The scent of pure bullshit is so strong in the room that Billet's nose wrinkles instinctively from the smell. He rolls his eyes only to find Largo stares straight at him.

"Is there a problem with that, Captain?"

It is his turn to be focused on.

"I understand you and your crew tried to assist when the enclosure went down: fired into the crowd, further stirring the confused citizens into a frenzy." Largo states as if reading off a list of criminal charges.

"With all due respect, sir, everyone started firing when the Zees came over the fence," Billet replies.

"Citizens." Largo corrects him.

Jake respects the undead for what they are: flesh-eating killing machines. He understands the city wants to protect their own, thus the enclosure around the entire west side of town. If it wasn't for the doped meat they fed them, the UCRA would be an army of Ferals, like the ones which roam the wilds outside town.

"His crew and vehicle were responsible for putting the collapsed fence line upright again until assistance arrived," the Colonel says. "We would've lost many more on both sides."

Jake appreciates Jackson standing up for him though he feels more a kid with a parent defending him when caught beating the neighbor's dog.

"We will go." Pike says, slaps a fist to his chest like a good Roman. "Captain Billet and I would be happy to do what needs to be done to appease the citizens of Grand Rapids."

Jake's eyes nearly fall from his head.

Pike sees his look and gives him a smug grin.

They both go blank faced when Jackson glances over his shoulder at them.

"We can do this." Jackson turns his gaze to Largo, the Mayor and the council members. He clasps his fingers together and rests his hands on the table.

"Colonel, I..." Billet starts to say.

"It would be much appreciated." Largo cuts in. "A good show of respect to the families and friends of the lost." His entire demeanor changes from pissed to sugar sweet.

Jake looks at Pike, who nods and grins, and then glances at the smug Rupert Largo. For an instant the City Treasurer stares straight at him with his one good eye. *Is the man really that happy with his win, or is there something else.* Jake thinks he suspects a hint of mischief in the man before Largo turns his attention to the mayor.

"Does that sound feasible, Mr. Mayor?" Largo says, fuzzy as a kitten.

Honeywell peers about the room, stops at his treasurer and brother-in-law, and nods. "It'll do. Make sure the Colonel's men are well compensated for their actions. This isn't punishment, it's a rescue mission. Whatever they need, the city will provide."

The people in the office area drop their fists and angry looks. Billet sees some hug each other. *Yes, obviously we were broadcasting*, shaking his head.

The mayor rubs his temples with the palms of his hands. "If there isn't anything else…" He shoots a look of irritation all about the room.

Heads shake, negative. No words.

Honeywell rises, reaches over and presses the intercom switch with such force the button doesn't pop back up. He turns to Largo, growls at him. His brother-in-law towers over him as Dennis Honeywell is a short, slender man. But under the pale skin of his exposed arms, he is a coiled cable of muscle. Not a wimp or timid man, nor could he be in his present position and situation.

"You and I need to talk," he says to Largo, low but loud enough to be heard. "I have a meeting with Silas Regan." He says to the rest, without enthusiasm. "Lord knows what Reganshire is demands now."

Everyone stands as the mayor steps through a side door to his private office.

Largo waits until the door slams shut.

"We have four listed as missing on your report, Major." He says without missing a beat. "The Jenkin boys: Billy and Tommy, and Anthony and Julia Leonaldi,"

"Yes, sir." Pike stands at attention.

Jackson and Billet both look at Pike.

Suck up, Jake thinks, then realizes nothings been said about Rhino; the big Zee that crashed through the grunts with his following of four other missing zombs.

"There were five actually. This one big fella…" Billet chimes

45

in.

"According to Major Pike's report…"

"Confirmed, sir." Pike responds quickly. "Captain Billet is correct. There were five."

Jackson doesn't budge but his stare is on his clasped hands. His jaw line stands out, teeth clenched tight. He wants to chastise Pike, but doesn't.

Billet wonders what Jeremy's game is. The TC and his tank hadn't been in the vicinity until after the Rhino and his followers dropped into the drink. Any grunt Pike spoke to after the ordeal has to have told him about the undead behemoth who wade through them like a scythe through wheat stalks.

Jake decides to let it go. For now. Bone weary, he has no energy for any further arguing or finger-pointing.

"Captain Billet, are you up to this?" Largo asks, still annoyingly cheery. "The hero of Grand Rapids would again be looked upon favorably." The statement drips with sarcasm but is slathered with a true politician's honey.

Billet sours like he's ingested a mouthful of tart raspberries.

Jackson shakes his head and moans.

Pike sneers.

The City Treasurer sees the TC's reaction. His smile broadens.

Jake wonders if Largo knows about Pike's bitterness towards the subject.

The light in the room is suddenly too much to bear, stabs right through Jake's eye sockets. His shoulders slump. His head hurts; too much bullshit for one day already.

Jackson reads his fatigue.

"You have yourself a tank and a heavy transport. We'll need at least two small assault vehicles," Jackson says, writes his needs on a legal pad before him. He won't cast his team out on a rescue mission unprepared. "We'll be ready to roll as soon as all is taken care of." His pen marks a heavy period and he slides the paper across the table where it exchanges hands until it reaches Largo. The Treasurer picks it up, eye scans the script.

Largo's scarred brow furrows.

"This will take at least the rest of the day," he huffs. His fists clench. The paper crinkles.

The Colonel cracks a smile and sits back in his seat, arms across his chest. Billet hadn't seen what the man scribbled.

"My men need a little R&R before they head out on this jaunt," the Colonel says, crossed arms move higher up his chest. "And we aren't going out there, in current conditions, weather or otherwise, with popguns when you've been sitting on my weapon upgrades."

Largo looks at the crumpled paper in hand, and grumbles, "The people waiting on news of their loved ones won't be happy if they have to wait another day."

The Colonel turns his head to his two CO's. "Not like we'll bring them home, revived and back to their former glory," in a voice just loud enough for them to hear.

Billet keeps solemn faced.

Pike grins.

"It'll have to be, Mr. Largo." Jackson pushes his chair out and stands.

Meeting over, the rest of the council gets up, works their way to the doors, silent nods, no handshakes.

As Jackson is the first out of the meeting chamber, the citizens in the outer office area crowd him. "Nothing more to say." He waves them aside. "Please address your council members with any further comments or concerns."

Billet and Pike walk behind Jackson as he exits the office area and steps out into the hall. Jackson stops before the elevator that will bring them down to the ground level.

"No friends made today," Billet says, looks behind them. He expects torches, angry people and pitchforks to rush them.

"We may be on the city's payroll, but they don't own us."

"What did you request that Largo didn't like to pony up?" Pike asks.

The Colonel listens to the rattle and hum of the elevator as it rises to their location.

"Nothing for the tanks, Major. You guys got good armament, enough to deal with the outside world. But..." Jackson glances at Billet. "Before we lose further transports like the Huron and Ontario, City Council's been holding onto a few artillery modifications for our M213's."

Billet's eyes widen, surprised the deal has finally gone through.

"Is Phelps going to have issue with her rig experiencing a little open head surgery?" Jackson asks Jake.

The elevator pings. The doors slide open.

Though at the moment, feeling more dead than the west side *citizens*, Jake's face splits into a smile. "As long as our *patient* is stitched up and solid, I think she'll be fine with it."

Either that or Lou will have my balls for mirror dice.

***

"It's a beautiful day, isn't it, Jay?"

Jake feels the crush of his wife's hand press against his. They lay on a plaid blanket upon a lush green field of waving grass. The happy squeal and laughter of his son Joey catches his ears and he turns to see the five year old, arms waving, as the boy chases two white butterflies. Jake's old black and white terrier, Pandy, runs alongside the boy. She barks and yaps and nips at Joey's heels. Jake hasn't seen the old dog since he was a kid himself. It fills him with a warmth warmer than the summer sun to see the child and the dog at play.

"I will always love you," Jenna says with a brush of lips across Jake's cheek.

And then she is up and gliding away from him. Joey and the

terrier are alongside her, all three run over a green swell of grass and yellow flowers.

Jenna raises her slender hand to wave at Jake.

A bright flash. He squints, flinches, as the sun hits her diamond wedding band.

He blinks. Wife and child are gone. His childhood pet: gone.

The sun fades from the sky, turning the landscape to gray.

The tall grass curls in upon itself until it meets the ground. The withering blades turn into a vast carpet of cream-colored rice, grain that is not grain, but small, writhing vile things: a sea of twisting, squirming maggots.

Over the larval hill, a M1A3 Abrams growls into sight before a cloud of black dust. The big tank draws closer on every wave of the wriggling soil. Out of the trailing dark cloud shambles forth an army of the undead, the cloud itself a mass of black flies.

Billet's heart races as he tries to rise.

The picnic blanket beneath him turns burgundy. It changes from soft fabric to sticky syrup. He can't pull himself free.

The tank draws closer.

Riding in the TC's turret hatch, stands the Rhino Zee; its face a melted candle wax semblance of Jeremiah Pike. A dozen rotting Gurks stand or kneel about the turret, one of them Billet recognizes: Wills, the young soldier who'd been crushed and mauled to death.

Their bodiless heads stitched together by braided tow cable, like a grisly garland, Stokes, Mulholland, Campau and Loutonia hang across the cowl of the tank.

Jake fights to rise. Half snarls, half shrieks, tears roll from his eyes. A flood of emotions well up from within, yet no sound emits from his open mouth.

The Abrams crests the rise directly before him. The 120mm turret cannon is suddenly point blank in his face, so close he can make out the fine etch marks within the smoothbore gun barrel.

The gun fires in Billet's face in an overlapping repetition, far faster than its normal six rounds per minute capability.

Boomboomboomboom.

Jake snaps upright, soaked bed sheets roll to the floor. Disorientated, his eyes adjust to the room illuminated by dull daylight which comes through half drawn blinds.

"Jesus H." He runs his fingers through his sweaty strands of dark hair. *Still feel like shit,* but figures the fever (not fully realized he had until now) has broken.

Boomboomboomboom, the wood door thunders to his tiny living quarters.

For a heartbeat, the image of the dead, the tank and the rotting field fills his head.

"Captain?" A female voice calls from behind the door. "Jake? Are you in there?"

Loutonia.

Sliding out of his rack, he goes to the door. He grabs his pants off the back of his desk chair. Not that he necessarily needs them around his driver, yet they are on duty 24/7; other people could be with her.

He turns the deadbolt and latch handle at the same time and opens the door.

It's only her.

"Come in." He steps aside to let her by, peers left and right down the hallway. Their barracks are in a refurbished office building. The entries to each soldier's quarters stand far apart, the dingy carpet and dusty fake plants the only other occupants in the corridor.

"I'd been out there for a bit pounding and calling," Loutonia says as she flips on the main room light.

Billet shuts the door, turns and squints as if a spotlight has been thrown in his face.

"You must've been dead to the world." Loutonia looks about

the room as she steps deeper within. Other than the bathroom, the place is all one room: living room and bedroom (a foldout cot) and kitchenette. "I was ready to kick down the door."

The HTV driver stands at Billet's height, even without combat boots. She is not a small, frail thing by any stretch, and Jake is sure if she wanted to come through the dense wood door, she wouldn't be stopped.

"I wasn't feeling too well. I still feel a bit under the weather." Billet rubs the back of his neck. His calloused fingers play across raised scar tissue from too many close quarter encounters in the field.

"Oh?" concern in the woman's voice. She turns and puts a hand to Jake's head.

He flinches; the red scar that runs from temple to temple burns at her touch.

Only for a moment.

He closes his eyes. Loutonia's hand is cool and smooth, soothing, against his forehead.

"You're still warm." Loutonia moves a little closer. She purses her lips to kiss his cheek.

He turns, cocks head away before she can touch him.

"Better not," he says and then takes her hand before she backs away from the rebuff. "I don't want you to get whatever I have… if it's contagious."

Her frown turns into a smile and she moves close. "You could be on the edge of Turning and I wouldn't avoid you," she says.

She presses her full, dark lips against his which feel dry and thin. He does not try to stop the action this time, but groans a bit within as it is only a short kiss.

There is more. She flicks her eyelashes along his neck and cheek as she moves to his ear. "Oh, and I do need to tell you about my thoughts on the Huron's upgrade," she whispers, hot breath in his ear. "They worked all night on it. They made quite a mess of my baby," she says referring to the carrier.

Jake tenses, waits for a knee to the balls.

"I love it," she says, no hint of anger or annoyance. No knee to the groin.

He relaxes and, feels the urge to take her to bed.

She moves back, sees the look in his eyes, and grins.

"Now go take a shower, Captain, sir." She playfully pushes him away. "You look and smell like ass."

She goes to the small kitchenette, and begins to rummage about for the coffee and his antique percolator.

Feeling dejected, he shakes his head to dispel the... thoughts.

Bad move. The head shake. Makes his skull hurt like his brain is loose, slaps back and forth, a steel ball in a bone cage.

Shouldn't be thinking about that shit anyway, damn job to do.

"We're ready to roll as soon as you are. Campau's got the manifest from one of Pike's guys. They have us staying on the river's west side, heading along Butterworth. Vets Memorial Drive if possible," Jake hears Loutonia say as he heads into the bathroom.

The lavatory had been a literal broom closet back in the day. Outfitted with a toilet, a tiny sink and a walk-in shower, the lemon-yellow paint on the walls threatens to peel off in sheets. He doesn't close the door fearing the sagging plasterboard ceiling might come down on his head as he showers and he'll have to make a quick escape.

As he checks himself in the small oval mirror, Jake watches Loutonia pull a coffee can from the cabinet above the kitchen sink. She pops the lid, looks inside, makes a sore face and tosses the empty container in the trash.

"It rained all night. The whole southwestern edge of the UCRA is way underwater now. That'll make for a fun time," Loutonia says, the clatter of her rummaging continues as he turns on the shower and disrobes.

The nozzle head spits a drizzle of water before it blasts to life.

Jake steps in, lets the initial cold water pelt him. He shivers, takes it, until the warmth comes.

The sting between the cold and the hot further wakens him, snaps his senses alive, lets him know he is not in that wicked dream but back into the usual hell. He feels more in control of the wakeful moments, considering. It's hard to control the ghosts of nightmares, of memories, even if it stems from the bite of fever.

"What do you think is up with Pike?" Loutonia pops her head inside the bathroom.

She tries to peer over the condensation haze the steam makes against the glass shower door. Jake frowns at her as they make visual. She backs out as he soaps up.

"Something," Jake says, feeling the raised lines of scar tissue as he scrubs himself down. Arms, legs, chest, face, head: he has more lines than a mile of freeway. "I haven't seen him much since we returned home. I hear he's been doing several runs to Reganshire and Allendale."

"Happy to follow in our footsteps."

"I think he'd feel better if he had the opportunity to erase our footsteps."

Jake lets the water rinse the soap away, along with some of the fatigue. "Grand Rapids and our unit got lucky having the Major and the Devastator join our pack. When he plays with a level head, he's a strategic genius. He's pulled my fat from the fryer many a time back in the day."

Billet takes a breath, turns off the shower. The scalding water drips away as does the momentary exhilaration. Weariness starts to reform again like rust on bare metal.

"He's also got the biggest ego of the entire unit," Billet continues, "and he's itching to get me into a position to knock me down a peg or two. He's still jealous of me, of us, taking the Lettner mission."

"I remember it more as we were *assigned* the mission. No

choice. Here, you're doing it," Loutonia adds as she walks back across the room to the kitchenette.

Jake steps out of the stall, nods and wraps himself with a moth-eaten blue bath towel. "Pike's been trying to spread bullshit that I'm responsible for the current rise in the late regent's loyalist activities."

"You have to admit, all was pretty quiet until Muskegon executed that piece of work. The Sixth Street Dam bombing and the MORG factory attacks; unheard of before we did what we did." Loutonia stands before Jake's thigh-high refrigerator. She bends, opens the door. She huffs like she's been punched in the stomach, quickly shuts it.

"Speaking of the dead, you need to purge the biology experiment you got going on in here." She looks at Jake, nose wrinkled.

He ignores her ribbing. "We knew shit was going to happen. Didn't matter if we did what we did, or if it was Pike, Forrester, or someone else."

"I know Pike's a blowhard, but he really wants that kind of spotlight?"

Billet sniffs, nose running, as he pulls on fresh briefs, t-shirt and combat uniform, socks, boots, and then Kevlar tactical vest.

"He's bucking for promotion I figure," Jake says, "He knows Jackson is ready to step down sooner than later."

Fully geared up, he steps into the small living space. He grabs his holstered sidearm hanging on the back of the Salvation Army-bought couch. He pulls the P228 from holster, ejects the orange clip of nonlethals. Inserts a very lethal clip of .357 SIGs, re-holsters and straps on.

"Are we Oscar Mike?" Loutonia walks up to him, runs her dark calloused hand over his arm and shoulder. "Feeling better?"

He wants to kiss her.

She knows this. She casts a teasing smile as she continues

towards the door.

"Feeling better." Jake replies as he follows her. He shuts off the apartment lights and glances at the ruffled un-made bed still dark with sweat stains. "Yeah, I'm good to go."

It's a lie.

***

The door scanner flashes a red laser light over Billet's pocket insignia. With a sharp electronic beep, the locks disengage with a metallic wheeze. Dual steel doors slide open, rattling and squealing across a dirt-laced track. He walks wearily through them, nods salutation without words to the pair of soldiers pulling guard duty inside the bowels of GRCC vehicle garage.

The Van Andel Civic Center, once the premier venue for sporting events in Grand Rapids, is the home of the GRCC's Joint Maneuvers Compound. The expansive arena floor and the first tier seating area has been refurbished into a large service bay. The expanded floor space houses the Gurks few remaining Main Battle Tanks, Infantry Fighting Vehicles and HTV's while across the street in an old Ellis Parking ramp, the smaller vehicles are stored. The Arena's outer perimeters along the upper remodeled seating and suite levels hold quarters for the Commissioned Officers and NCO's.

A gaunt Lieutenant steps out from an office cubby to the left of a long hall leading to the main floor area. He salutes Billet in mid-stride, waves a clipboard thick with paperwork in his other hand.

"Good day, Captain. Good news. The new turret installation went off without a hitch." The lieutenant speaks as if the Huron has just come out of major surgery. "I am sure you will like what you see. Your crew has been briefed on its utilization."

As they walk down the corridor they pass closed and darkened doorways. The names of each office's former occupant remains etched in broad white letters upon the glass door pane.

"...basically a 25mm M242 Bushmaster chain-fed autocannon. The turret and body a bit smaller than the Bradley equipped variant. We tried to give you the 8 horsepower firing system, but the M213's electrical system is already maxed out..." The lieutenant rattles off the Huron's new armament capabilities while, paying little attention, Jake glances from the corner of his eyes at each name and each dark, empty office beyond.

"...so we have the 1hp system in there. Still have a ROF of 200 rounds per minute..."

Gunnery Staff Sgt. Ryan Pierce. Fellow new recruit with Billet during their inaugural military training. Friend. Mortally wounded during a recon patrol outside city limits April of last year.

"...remote-controlled through helmet-mounted HUD. It can be toggled between the cab, the front gunner's and your commander's control systems..."

Lt. Major James Piegeon. ACAV CO. Joey and his son used to play together while Jenna and Piegeon's wife chewed their nails while the men were out poking Feral beehives with sticks that go boom. Succumbed to the Blight Christmas 2023.

"...gun has a new suppression system so you can nearly stand next to without blowing your eardrums out. Shortens your firing range, but if you can't hit a target at 1500 metres..."

Captain Lambert Rigley. Commander of HTV Ridgerunner Superior. Helped Billet get his current vehicle command early on. Friend. Commander, crew and vehicle lost on an Eastern Michigan run March of this year. A month ago.

"Damn," Jake groans, shakes his head.

"Yeah, I know. Awesome, right?" The lieutenant chirps like an excited school girl, still reading off his clipboard.

The Colonel's office: located center of the hallway. Jackson had taken over for Renald Neilsen, another good man who had fallen to the Blight while Jake had been ferrying William Lettner out of town.

Pike's tank battalion office sat next to Jackson's. At least Billet and Forrester, the commander of Ridgerunner Ontario, hadn't been dumped into Jeremy's bucket after Piegeon's passing. But Jake feared if the Colonel removed himself from the picture, and if Pike succeeds him…

"…couldn't give you the full accompaniment of AP or HE loads, but you have enough firepower to put a hurt on someone. A lot of someones."

Billet continues forward.

The Lieutenant stops. It is then he realizes Jake may have not been fully listening. He clears his throat which comes out more like a balloon rapidly losing air.

Jake stops.

The Lieutenant rushes up to his side, continues. "Only have one TOW tube. We're trying to add some to our BRV-O fleet, but you have a four missile load-out just the same."

The clipboard flashes up under Jake's nose.

"Sign here, here and here." The Lieutenant points.

Billet absently takes up the pen dangling from a string attached to the clipboard, signs the weapons change out/change over receipt papers.

"Damn, kid, were you a car salesman in your prior life," Jake says under his breath.

"What was that, sir?"

"Never mind."

The last door on the right of the hallway: Captain J. Billet, in small white letters splayed across the upper face of the glass pane; below the name, a vinyl American flag decal.

Facing Billet, the Lieutenant steps back with the signed documents. He brushes against the sensor pad on the aluminum doorframe. It blinks red, angrily beeps at him.

Jake winces, the sound a knitting needle jab to his temples.

He steps up and leans into the pad so his pocket insignia is read by the scanner.

The pad beeps, flashes a green light. A series of bolts withdraw into the sturdy frame, and the door visibly loosens from its rigid state.

"Your additional cargo is also onboard," the Lieutenant says rolling back the last document for signature.

More Z-rations, Billet assumes and absently scribbles his signature. He misses the look on the other man's face: nervous, bomb dropped, wanting to get away before things go boom look.

The tense moment passing, the Lieutenant goes military rigid, clicks his heels together and salutes. "Thank you, sir. I'll inform your crew you're clear to go."

Jake waves the soldier on and steps into the cool, dark confines of his office.

***

Lights remain off.

Head remains pounding.

Jake sits for a moment in his squeaky desk chair, elbows on the dusty desktop, forehead in upraised palms. Through slit eyes, he casts a glance at the dust-fogged picture of his late wife Jenna and son Joey. Joey was 16 in the picture. It was the last full year Jake spent with either of them before being sent to Lansing. It was during his SOC (Special Operations Command) training the Blight washed full force across the country and globe.

Joey would have been 24 years old this year. 16 seems eons ago.

Jake's fingers gently play across the head wound he'd received in the wilds last Fall; it feels like a hot worm laying across his forehead. One of many "war wounds" received in the field, the vaccine and fast meds in every instance kept him from death.

He feels like shit now, and wonders.

"Every soldier is different." A medic in Milwaukee told him while they were there this past winter. "No one knows really how long the vaccine stays in one's system."

Perhaps I've pushed myself too far, he thinks.

On his desk phone, a red message light glows. The dull light even hurts his eyes. With being out in the field so much, he is surprised the message remains, all these years it hasn't been deleted or erased.

A shaky finger arches down and partially presses the call retrieval button.

"Captain, you need to come out here on the double," Phelps voice snaps in Jake's earbud.

Ah shit, he thinks, *here comes the crotch kick. She's pissed I let them muck with the Huron.*

"I'll be right there," he replies, taps the new ear piece.

He bolts upright from his chair.

Too fast.

The room tilts sideways. He grabs the back of the seat and lets the dizziness fade.

"That's awesome. Just awesome." He says to himself.

He straightens his shirt, makes sure he isn't going to topple, and heads out of the room. The service bay is a short distance away.

As the office door clicks shut behind him, and dead bolts mechanically ka-chunk into place, the old phone message plays to the empty room. "Jacob. It's Jenna. I am sorry about the argument. I understand completely. I'm just scared. For you. For us. But know I'll always support you. Do what you have to do for you. Do what you have to do to keep pushing on. Just don't...forget us."

***

It's not the 25mm cannon turret welded and wired to the top of the Huron. It's not the new piece of weaponry that takes up half of the space where the roof-top cargo hatch had been. It isn't any of that which causes the upset tone in Loutonia's voice.

Campau stands in Jake's command hatch, wears the special tanker's helmet with the remote sensors. Left, right, left, right, up, down. The gun turret effortlessly moves with his head motions.

Stokes stands on the concrete floor beside the Huron. He greedily gnaws on a stump of cigar lodged in the corner of his mouth, eyes on the new weaponry. There is eagerness in his look— narrow eyed and big mischievous grin.

"Down, boy." Jake says as he walks by his front gunner. *Mental note: make sure the man is thoroughly versed, and thensome, before letting him get his hands on the gun.*

Loutonia and Mulholland meet Billet in the rear of the Huron, the back ramp down. Phelps wears an annoyed sneer against Mulholland's forlorn look, though Jake isn't sure if those are aimed at him or the additional people at the back of the rig.

Councilman Leon Sutter, his wife Julia, and another couple Billet doesn't recognize stand with his two crew members.

Mrs. Sutter weeps, as does the other woman; great sobs make their shoulders bounce. They look groupies from an Alice Cooper concert; eyes and cheeks streaked black with mascara lines.

"Take care of our boys, Captain." Leon Sutter says, he looks ready to breakdown himself. "They know they did a stupid thing, but please make sure they get to their destination safely."

Jake squints into the gloomy guts of the open transport.

His eyes adjust.

Sutter's son and son's buddy sit on the metal seat pans, staring down at their sneakers. Backpacks stuffed to the gill lay at their feet.

Additional cargo, the Lieutenant had said, as Jake signed one extra traveler manifest.

He winces as another lancing pain needles through his temples.

At least, this time, he knows the cause.

Chapter Four
The Wet Shall Inherit the Earth

The rain departs, leaves the sky cloudless and clear. The sun shines down. Beautiful, except the land below the bright blue firmament has become a massive lake. West and south of the overly engorged Grand River rest under several feet of water.

Jake dons tinted goggles, helps with the glare from the sky, the glare from the sun hitting the water's surface. He feels surprisingly good standing in his commander's hatch. He can tell a slight fever still simmers within, but a cool breeze blows across the Huron's body. It is like a wave of freshness. Invigorates. Exhilarates.

He wants to laugh at all the bullshit in the world, but doesn't.

He suspects Phelps ordered up more than "headache medicine" in the medi-pack cocktail. Campau had said nothing upon injecting him as they left the city, though Jake recalls the young man wore a poorly hidden shit eating grin on his mug.

A knot tension at the base of his neck is the only irritant at the moment. The throbbing temples are gone. Jake's focus is clear. His mood almost as bright as the stabbing sun.

It's a good thing at this point.

"I wonder when Noah's coming?" Loutonia says over the comm as she takes the Huron through its umpteenth "puddle."

The water ripples high enough to tickle the rear track drive wheels. "Perhaps we should've suggested guys with Coast Guard or Navy training to roll with us."

Campau breaks in. "It isn't the water that's freaking me. How many UCRA civilians are in here? Twenty-five thousand or something? It's creepy how quiet the neighborhood is. It's so... dead."

"Are you kidding me?" Stokes responds. "Come on, kid. Is that all ya got?"

"What? Oh." Campau realizes what he's said. "I meant, figuratively."

The majority of the UCRA still remains amassed near the downtown area. None of the Zees seem tempted to wade into the flooded neighborhoods. Deeper into the west side the place is a ghost town. Typical runs through the enclosure, the resident undead wander the streets, homes and buildings. It is commonplace to hear them crashing and banging into things and speaking in whatever dialect they emit between them. All around the convoy the neighborhood is silent, eerie, even against the hum and growl of the armored motorcade.

"Ole Bob is even staying inside," Jake says under his breath as they pass the rundown Marathon Gas Station. The old 1950's era "satellite Zee" the GRCC uses for Intel isn't at his usual corner post. No dirt and blood-stained ancient attendant in blue coveralls waves at them or coaxes them in for a 25 cent fill-up or white wall tire sale.

For being in such a state of brain-rot, Billet is surprised they don't see any floaters, or residents marooned in or around their dilapidated property.

Even the undead know when to stay out of the rain.

"Deep dip in the road coming up," Campau says across the closed frequency channel only the Huron crew is privy to.

"Victor One and Two, we have a dip in the road. Close up

formation," Billet says as *his* open channel goes out to the two Humvee BRV-O's trailing behind the Huron.

"Victor One and Two forming up," the lead Gurk in the first vehicle, Enrique Leonardson, responds in return. With his right hand hanging out the open window, Leonardson gives Billet a thumbs-up as the Humvee starts to draw closer to the rear of the big transport.

All vehicles stop, bumper to bumper. Soldiers from each toss tow straps to the other and hook them around appropriate ring or draw bar. In short order, the Huron becomes the mother duck with two adolescents roped behind her.

With a jerk, they move forward into the flooded section of roadway.

Exhausts on the BRV-O's extend straight up, chrome horns growing out their front quarter panels. Good thing as the water comes up to the bottom of the LTV's doors as they cut through the Huron's broad wake. The 18-inch vehicle ground clearance is nothing as they hit the deepest section of the swamped road. The water line splashes at the smaller vehicle's quarter panels as 26-inch wheels come close to submersion.

"Wakeboarding with dingle berries," Stokes says on the Huron's closed frequncy.

"I'll open broadcast and see what our trail mates think of being called shit balls," Campau warns, not yet used to Stokes crude humor.

The Huron's twin diesels rev. Phelps keeps a straight course down the center of the two-lane street. Unable to see the dividing line under the watery murk, she drives by memory. She's traversed the roadway so many times the potholes read like Braille. She knows exactly where they are along the stretch of road.

The Humvees follow suit. They accelerate to keep pace with the transport, not wanting to be pull toys for very long.

A massive arch of water splays out on either side of the

Huron. It sends churning waves over submerged sidewalk and front yards. Old homes and buildings along Bridge Street stand with open entryways and the Huron-generated tides rush into their wood and aluminum-framed maws.

The depression in the roadway is a short span. Jake glances over the side of the Huron as the rear tracks climb out of the small lake. A shower of water weeps off the vehicle's protective skirting in line with the upper bogies. It is nothing for the Huron to plow through, but seepage into the engine compartments and the rear ramp could be a real problem. He sees other "puddles" that appear much deeper down side streets judging by the old abandoned cars and trucks with rooftops barely poking above the water line.

"This is fucking ridiculous." Exclamation comes from the open radio channel. Jake recognizes the irritated voice of Todd Riley in the rearmost Humvee: Victor Two.

"Leave your windows down?" Billet asks over the comm.

"Didn't have to," Riley replies. "Got hit by the backwash and knocked our visors off. I don't have an issue with indoor swimming pools, but we didn't bring suits."

"I'll try to get the Apostolate on the horn and see if they have dry gear for you." Billet thinks it might have been a better idea to have brought extra clothing.

"You'll look good in some old rotter's pants." Leonardson chuckles.

"We'll switch positions on the way to Butterworth, Lennie." Riley warns, returns Leonadson's humorous jab. "We'll see how you guys like it."

"I got movement at three o'clock." Stokes breaks over the comm as the vehicles slow and tow lines are disengaged.

Mulholland scrambles back to the rear gunner's hatch, one of Huron's tow straps cradled in arm before Stokes finishes his statement.

Billet hears the hum of their new 25mm turret as it starts

to come online. He turns his head left in the direction Stokes has indicated.

"Stand down on the big gun," Jake says.

Campau responds: "Roger that, Captain." The cannon winds down.

Jake looks beyond Stokes and his deadly quad machine gun bundle. He notices a lone figure north of them at the far end of Pettibone Avenue. They are already passing the street. It is not worth Phelps to stop and back up.

Jake taps his earbud, mutes the transmission pickup to not blow the eardrums out of his crew.

"Whatcha got?" He says to Stokes across the roof. He can see the figure in the distance but already a line of trees—then houses—obscure his view.

"It's a local, moving on the same westerly course as us, following the expressway." Stokes says, continues to scan the area as the next block of house cuts his view.

A block over: the I-196 expressway, the northern boundary of the UCRA enclosure. The old freeway is one of the dividing lines for the west side of Grand Rapids. The raised and fence-lined roadway wraps around the entire extended neighborhood. It starts at the Grand River, in the north eastern crotch of Interstate 196 and 131, drops south then southwest where Market Avenue meets the 196 river overpass. On the northern side of the enclosure, the fence line follows the contour of 196 until it hits Butterworth. The weed choked and rutted interstate is lined all the way round with 15-foot fencing topped with coiled concertina wire on the UCRA side. Parts of the opposing fence, some sections electrified, keep the hungry and unsociable out, and the Grand Rapids undead citizenry in.

"I lost him," Stokes remarks, swivels the quads forward.

Billet scratches at a small scar on his chin. "What was it carrying? I thought I spied something for the brief instant I got a look."

Gun-toting Zees within the UCRA isn't uncommon, though the GRCC disarms them when found. There is a suggestion, not acted on, to corral all the citizens and do a thorough search of all abandoned homes and businesses. No one is signing up for the job.

There is nothing worse than a zombie with a gun though. It gave a whole new meaning to the term "wild fire."

"It had… something… for sure. A rifle?" Stokes replies, eyes still on the passing homes and side yards. "And it was either the Hunchback of Notre Dame or humping a big ole backpack."

"Incoming call from the Apostolate, Captain," Campau says.

"Patch her in," Jake responds, expects the good Sister Mirose on the other end.

A female voice comes over the airwaves along with the rapid pop of machine gun fire, screams, shouting.

"Captain Billet, what's your ETA?" the frantic woman asks on the other end.

It isn't Mirose.

"The Apostolate is under attack. I repeat. We're under attack."

***

"Don't hit the people in the street," Jake says over the comm. Bullets ping off the hatch coaming. He ducks within the cupola.

"Roger that," Phelps responds. "Where do you want me to park?"

Stokes grips the handles of his quad 30's. His fingers quiver with anxiousness as he wants to send a hail of hot lead into their adversaries. He laughs, takes a moment to give the attacker's a middle finger salute.

He is rewarded with a shot tearing a gash across his upper arm. "Muthafuckers!" He slips like a stumpy gopher into his hatchway, hairy fists off his gun. For now.

On open channel, Jake says: "Put us at a 45 in front of the Apostolate. Keep the fire off the building. Victor One and Two, form up behind me but keep distance to maneuver. Watch our undead citizenry; they're in a bit of a frenzy."

Bridge Street runs east and west, gradually sloping upward at the corner of Bridge and Valley where the West Side Apostolate is located. Roughly 200 feet from the corner, on the hill, the I-196 expressway overpass looms. Where the fence and razor should tower, peeled back metal links open a large gap in the enclosure. A dozen armed men perch with helmet, body armor and faces hid behind red handkerchiefs. The invaders fire down at the Apostolate and the newly arrived GRCC in a bullet storm which rivals yesterday's rainy downpour.

Those aren't Reganshire men I hope. Jake's heard the small town guard wear colors now.

He drops down into the Huron's guts. Phelps angles the vehicle in and stops as he pulls the hatch shut behind him lest someone from above dunk a lucky lead shot down their throat.

The new 25mm gun turret hums as it traverses; Billet steps around the rotating body as he grabs an assault rifle from its wall cradle. With a SCAR 556 in hand, he moves to the rear of the vehicle.

"I can brush the assailants off the overpass," Campau says in Jake's earbud, manning the turret remotely inside the front cab.

"Negative. We take this one outside," Jake responds. Stokes still swears as he drops to the steel deck behind him.

Scotty Sutter and his buddy, Lance Winthrop, glance up at Billet as he goes by, their eyes big as saucers. They hug their seat harness like they're on a coaster ride.

Jake nods at the youths with a crooked smile. "Welcome to summer camp." He palms the rear ramp release button.

Mulholland drops beside him from the rear gunner's hatch as the hydraulics moan and the ramp crunches to the cobbled asphalt roadbed.

"I have a clear shot." Campau says, excited, way too eager to fire the cannon.

"Negative. We can't afford more bad PR with the City."

Jake peers around the edge of the Huron's rear track guard, shakes his head. The action causes his temples to throb anew. He doesn't like what he sees and doesn't like the implications.

People enjoy doing a lot of things with the undead.

For the military, if a soldier isn't blown to little red bits; it is experimentation and the life of a ZT, zombie trooper.

For an undead neighbor, family or friend, within the city limits; they unknowingly find themselves protected and fed until they fall to the elements or rot to nothing and dissolve to a gooey paste.

Outside the civilized areas; it is a free-for-all. The living and the unloving have to fend for themselves, kill or be killed.

Billet understands why ZT's are captured and smuggled into other towns and villages. They can still be led, programmed to an extent, and are fierce, deadly and resilient fighting machines.

Jake leans out from the track cowling, fires at the men on the overpass, avoids three undead citizens who dangle by ropes halfway between the street and the highway above. Why the thugs are trying to snag the dead and decaying, and haul them up and away…

…It can't be good.

Mulholland leans out as Billet retracts. The gangly young gunner fires once, and Jake peers out to see one of the attackers start to topple forward, his face a crimson mess. Before the man goes over, two of his fellows grab him and thrust him down behind them.

"Yeah, don't let him get into our hands." Jake says aloud, squeezes off a few rounds towards the overpass. "We'll strip you down to see where you gents come from."

A yelp from the Humvee behind them snaps his attention to their immediate vicinity.

The Apostolate stands on somewhat high ground compared

to the rest of the surrounding neighborhood. It is an island in the midst of the west side flood waters. It is no wonder another large group of the UCRA gather about Mirose's place. The Zees who do not flounder with gunshot wounds, if the others were in some state of calm around the good sister's facility, the fighting and the noise stirs them like a hive of angry bees.

Leonardson and crew fight not only being targets for the overpass gang, but also the shambling citizenry who press into them as bullets fly.

A young woman with a few strands of dark hair sticking out of her skinless head walks with a purposeful gait straight into Enrique's outstretched gun hand. She hisses and claws at him up close and very personal. The Humvee commander can't twist his gun about to incapacitate her.

One of his men jumps to his aid. With the butt of his gun, he knocks her in the head. She teeters, staggers back a few drunken steps, and falls to the ground.

"Thanks for tha…" Leonardson starts to say when his savior's head suddenly snaps back. A red hole appears in the grunt's forehead as his helmet kicks off his skull. Blood and gray matter blow out the backside.

Billet watches, ignores the concrete erupting around him, as his team struggles more with the frenzied UCRA than the armed interlopers.

Jake sees a nun step from the Apostolate doors with an ancient musket. An old woman, he is reminded of the actress/comedian Betty White. With the Huron shielding her, she raises the old rifle, fires. The kick nearly puts her down on her ass. He sees a man and his buddy atop the overpass topple backwards. They do not rise.

Another sister comes through the door, hefts a big black crossbow to her shoulder and fires while her musket-wielding companion reloads.

Jake and Stokes back up Mulholland as he rushes to aid

Leonardson and Riley's team. They fire simultaneously making several of the overpass shooters fall back.

To the far left, one of the poor rotters who dangles, lassoed under the arms, jerks violently. The men who hold him fumble with the rope as they try to avoid the spray of lead and shrapnel coming off the concrete guard rail. The vicious bounce loosens the dead man's lower extremities. Pale and decay-eaten with gaping red holes, a leg drops with a meaty ka-thlop onto the roadway below.

"God *damn* them!"

Billet turns to see Sister Mirose step from the Apostolate's interior.

The big nun's right arm is held in a bloody sling. Yet still able to carry the weight, she comes out with a M60 machine gun and loose bandolier of bullets across her broad, full chest. Peppered with blood stains, her white shirt sleeves are rolled to the shoulder. They bulge with the square outline of cigarette packs. Her habit lies akimbo on her head, revealing sprigs of short shorn dark hair.

"The abduction of our innocent brothers and sisters will not be today," she snarls.

Bullets bite at the sidewalk all around her.

"Sister…" Jake starts to say, afraid he's going to see the woman gunned down.

She steps from behind the Huron, brings the machine gun up in one thick vein-lined arm, and unloads on the would-be kidnappers above.

"Back her up!" Jake yells as he and his team follow suit.

Bullets rain in a vertical downpour, but the lead droplets angle up, not down, and the overpass gang falls back.

Ropes go slack, the undead captives released. The three bodies hanging twenty feet off the ground drop to the pavement. Hard. They splatter. Bones shatter like glass.

The gun shots cease.

Truck engines rev amidst angry and agonized shouts. Jake

watches two full-size pickups speed away eastbound on the old interstate.

"Contact Central Command," he shouts over the comm. "Tell them to be on the lookout for two pickup trucks heading eastbound on I-196."

"Roger." Campau replies in Jake's earbud, though the young navigator steps from the rear of the Huron with Phelps; both drag a crate of Z-rations behind them.

More nuns rush from the building. They move directly into the throng of still-mewing undead. The BRV-O crews, those still standing, watch in awe as the local citizens calm almost on sight and smell of the reverent Sisters. Crates and cans open. Z-rations get immediately dispensed.

Jake looks about and sees Sister Mirose and the Betty White nun with musket-type long rifle. The two nuns rush to the downed Zees who lay in the street below the quiet overpass.

"What's happened here?" Billet says. He moves to Mirose while he casts a quick cautious eye to the bullet-chipped roadway above in case anyone lingers.

With the M60 on the ground, Mirose kneels over the broken body of the Zee who'd lost its leg. It lays in a heap, folded over at the waist, a closed book. The head is cracked where it hit the pavement. Thick burgundy sludge oozes from the broken skull. The Amazonian nun gently straightens the body, and then cradles the battered head against her bosom. She runs her leathery hand over the white eyes, closes the lids.

"Sister, there'll be time to take care of these bodies later. I need information." Billet watches Musket Nun delicately handle the two other bodies, placing tattered arms at sides, straightening twisted legs.

Two other nuns trot up with stretchers, clean white sheets folded squarely atop the gurneys. One of the women stifles a whimper as she sees the body Sister Mirose holds.

Mulholland and Stokes walk up behind Billet as he bends closer, hears Mirose mumbling.

"Sister..."

An index finger snaps up to silence him. Her attention doesn't leave the dead Zee.

"...and bless those, Lord, who have fallen now into true slumber, and take them into the Realm of Light and Peace, and into the Community of Your Saints."

Mirose's great frame shudders as her head droops lower.

"Eternal God, in your fatherly kindness, be good to the soul of your servant, Monsignor Robert Sullivan Pettish, who did so much in Your name when others would not."

Jake's stands up straight, goes rigid as he removes his helmet and holds it to his chest.

Mulholland, seeing his suddenly somber commander, does the same.

Stokes simply peers at the big nun cradling the ruined body. His face crinkles in disgust. Jake snarls at him. He removes his helmet.

"For this we pray, Our Lord. Amen."

The two nuns with the gurney make the Sign of the Cross as Mirose stands, lifts the dead man without effort. She places him on the stretcher and covers the body with white linen.

"That is... Father Pettish?" Jake says as the nuns carry the litter back towards the Apostolate. They pass the civilian Zees who sniff the air after them. Another nun quickly waves a fist full of the drugged meat slop, draws the civilians to her. "He resided over the mass at my wife and son's funeral." Jake finishes.

"It is a small world." Mirose dusts her black vest with her left hand then re-adjusts her right which has slipped from the sling during her activity. "Getting smaller."

Billet notices the wrap of surgical bandage on her forearm, several spots of red bleed through.

"We ran a little low on food with the flooding and, um, the refugees got a little hungry," Mirose sees Jake's eyes upon her arm. "I'll be fine. Lord willing."

Billet watches the nuns attend to the other two dead-dead Zees. Stokes rushes to assist as thick blond tresses unpile from beneath the fallen habit of one of the consecrated attendees. Behind them, the Gurks pick up the bullet-ridden bodies of those shamblers caught in the crossfire and distribute the meat slop to the survivors. Mulholland and Campau man the gun mounts on the Huron. They continue to scan the expressway above.

"I'm sorry for the loss of Father Pettish," Billet says to Mirose as they walk behind the litters carrying the dead. "I didn't even know he had turned."

"He was a great man. He started these aid stations for our downtrodden. People may turn their nose up at what is left of our citizens, but until their final destination," she says as she casually glances up at the black smoke rolling out of the Apostolate's rear chimney, "These people would be far more trouble for everyone if our missions weren't here."

They stop beside the Huron. Phelps emerges from the rear of the transport hauling supplies with the help of Scotty and Lance. For a moment, Mirose looks at the two young men, but turns full attention to the Huron's cocoa-skinned driver.

"Your two charges, Scott Sutter and Lance Winthrop." Billet nods towards the boys. "Their parents are more of a wreck than them, so..."

"We just received the communication this morning via Sister Clarissa's short wave," Mirose says, exchanges a nod with a stick-figure of a nun. The thin woman directs an undead bag of bones with more meat on his dilapidated frame than hers. "We'll take good care of them."

"So what can you tell me about this attack?" Billet asks.

"This attack?" Mirose says as if he should know. "This is the fourth time we've been attacked and those…slavers…have tried to snatch up some of our people."

"Fourth time? Why didn't you report this?"

"Our main radio has been down for two months. The last drop off your guys did—Commander Forrester and one of your loud-mouth tank commanders—one of the tank jockeys *tried* to fix the radio, but I swear mucked it up even worse." Mirose watches Loutonia and the two boys come out of the Apostolate. "And the storms garbled our signal to transmit over the short wave."

Jake nods, understands, determined to bring the subject up when he again meets with a certain "loud-mouth" TC.

"We did send communications to the city council. Word back, Rupert Largo was looking into it," Mirose says.

"I've heard of this," Jake responds, runs two fingers up under his helmet to massage his throbbing temples. "Unsavory types abducting Zees for illicit activities. Hell, we're hearing more and more of drug traffickers who use them for deliveries." He thinks of the handheld device Pike had shown him. "If this is the case, I'm surprised they're getting the balls to try this so close to the city."

"Desperate days, Captain. And we've always been the kind to find opportunity even in times like these," the good sister says.

Jake scratches at his chin. *We equals human beings.* He knows exactly what she's saying.

"Campau," he turns and calls up to the navigator manning Stoke's typical position. "What's Central had to say about the hostiles we drove their way?"

Campau appears at Huron's roof edge. "Sir, I've been unable to get through. We don't appear to have a signal. Anymore. Period."

Billet looks up at him.

"I can't say we've ever had a signal as this was the first time I've tried," Campau says. "I know everything was green this morning. I'm getting only some pulsing static, could be a jamming broadcast."

"Look into it, please." Jake says. "Try to hail the M45 outpost.

Benson's got the heavy gear. There's a HAM inside the Apostolate if need be."

Mirose nods her okay with his statement.

Perhaps he should have waved a hand for upgraded electronics versus the new weaponry for the HTV's. *Late to the table as usual,* Jake thinks.

"The pulse I'm getting will scramble the HAM too," Campau again. "I'll see what I can do though, sir." He finishes quickly, seeing his commander's sour look, and disappears back over the roof line.

"I have tools to patch up that fence," Jake offers the sister, feeling his temples start to throb. A drummer with sticks made of sledgehammers bangs at his head.

"That'd be much appreciated," Mirose says as she spies one of her sisters struggling with a slightly agitated, large Zee. "I think it might be frowned upon to see any of us do such a job," she finishes and heads off to help the other nun with the big zombie.

Billet nods, though he is sure the good Sister could tie the fence in a triple knot if she wanted.

"Got some way deep water ahead," Sergeant Riley says, walks up from a foray south down Valley Avenue. Valley would be their next venture to meet up with Pike at the Butterworth Test Facility.

Billet can only assume Pike has tried to radio for their Sitrep, or situational report. He inwardly smiles.

Riley and two of his crew members stand with wet uniform, the moisture lines goes to their waist. The vehicle commander holds a long tree branch he'd acquired on their jaunt, it shows the water line on it. It's longer than his arm.

"Our vehicles won't be able to be pulled through that," Riley says, shrugs.

Jake looks over Riley's shoulder, peers down street. He can't see the roadbed below the water. Deep, yes. The Huron can plow through it, but even then, if they hit a major depression, the rig might float like driftwood.

Jake responds: "We can take it from here then. You and Lennie can assist the Sisters. And if our friends come back," he nods towards the overpass, "feel free to Swiss Cheese them and ask questions later."

"Not a problem." Riley salutes.

"And I think they have the aforementioned dryer in there." Billet nods towards the Apostolate, dons a brief smile.

Riley and the two troopers silently return the gesture.

"You okay, Jake?" Loutonia asks, steps up beside him. Behind her, the two boys carry their rucksacks into the building.

"Could this day get any worse?"

Stokes wanders out of the Apostolate almost in a stagger. He holds the side of his face where a hand print blushes on his cheek.

"I think I got a date," the gunner chuckles.

The little blond-haired nun peers out around the corner of the door, waves her middle finger at him.

"We're all gonna go to Hell," Jake mumbles to himself.

***

"This thing proved pretty air tight," Campau says over the comm. "If we'd have conked out, I don't think the Coast Guard would be coming this far inland."

"I welded most of her plates up myself long before I thought we'd have to go naval," Loutonia responds.

The Huron pushes through water which rises to the top of the tracks. Its front end wants bounces as the big air-full front tires create buoyancy. Phelps manages to keep them going forward through the wet and thick of it, and brings them to a spot of dry pavement at Valley and Lake Michigan, four blocks south of the Apostolate.

"Great job, ma'am." Campau says to Phelps as she turns them west onto Lake Michigan. Other than a few shallow puddles, the roadway is easily navigable.

"Ma'am?" Loutonia replies, the mock hurt in her voice heard in everyone's earpiece. "I'm not that old."

Jake stands in the commander's turret, looks to the sky, wary of the gathering dark clouds. He shakes his head. *I'm tired of the rain already.* "Cut the chatter, people." He says. "Campau, have you been able to raise the BTF? They have to know what's going on here."

"Negative, sir, Butterworth isn't answering. I'm still receiving irregular feedback when I try to dial in the point of distortion jamming up everyone's signal."

"Keep trying."

They roll up the vacant street. Around a curve, along a small area of woods with trees that droop from all the precipitation, the M45 Outpost, the gateway to the untamed outskirts, came into view.

"Oh shit," Campau, Stokes and Mulholland say in unison.

"This… this is not good," Loutonia says. She brings the Huron to a stop at a point on the hill where Lake Michigan Drive merges into Fulton Street and becomes the *inner* state highway M45.

Stokes and Mulholland immediately leave their positions, climb down from the vehicle, guns in hand, and make their way up the street on foot.

"I don't care what you do or how you do it, Campau," Jake says, reaching down to grab the assault rifle in a stanchion just below his feet. "Get ahold of someone. Stat!"

Jake climbs out and down the side of the Huron. He catches up with Stokes and Mulholland as they stand at the inside gate of the M45 Outpost.

"Who do you think did this? Same guys we ran into at Mirose's? Another Loyalist attack? Reganshire?" Stokes says, boots crunching on a pile of roadway rubble.

Before them sits the M45 Outpost enclosure and small gatehouse. It partially stands, partially leans. The majority of it lays scattered here and there: flat, burnt, blasted and twisted. The guard shack and barracks made of galvanized sheet metal are scattered about like a spilled bag of potato chips. The street and nearby grounds have been chewed up by large munitions.

For several heartbeats, no one speaks.

"If I may comment, Captain," Mulholland asks to Billet's surprise.

Though Eddie is the less boisterous one of his gunner crew, the tall Southerner usually speaks his mind.

Billet nods him onward.

"Looking at the blast crater," Mulholland points at a large black furrow in the ground where a gate section had been, "the shot hit underneath the fencing. The discharge pattern suggests it came from the other side of the enclosure. It is a bit hard to tell, but that is what I see."

Stokes kicks at a piece of blackened sheet metal.

Jake realizes he sees no bodies.

"I thought Benson and crew were still here. I'm assuming they cleared out when they knew the water might cut off their route back to the city," he says, he still gazes about the wreckage, comforted somewhat by the lack of GRCC corpses. *Damn radio. I can't even call in to confirm or deny that statement or the situation.*

Mulholland moves ahead, walks the perimeter while Stokes pokes about in the blackened rubble.

"Commander, I traced the location of our signal disruption," Campau says in Jake's earbud. "I pinged off where the nearest signals emanate, triangulated their source, and dialed in, if you will, the stronger broadcast signals. It was kind of like cracking a safe by listening to the lock tumblers fall into place."

Jake ire rises beyond the boiling point. "Who's fucking with us?" he snaps, not able to bite his tongue with all the carnage around him.

"Sir, I have something over here." Mulholland waves Jake over to where he stands on a weed-choked patch of ground.

Campau responds: "Location is off Butterworth, southwest of the Butterworth Test Facility. The old gypsum mines."

"Some utility towers and a scant few broadcast towers out there, but, damn, that whole areas got to be underwater," Billet responds. "Do we have frogs mucking with our transmission lines?"

There is no outpost along that stretch of countryside; nothing between Grand Rapids, Walker and Grandville, friendly or otherwise. It doesn't mean someone couldn't set up a bit of chaos from out there. Everyone seems employed in the chaos business these days.

Jake stops beside Mulholland and looks down where the gunner points. He knows what the deep depression in the wet soil is but lets the gunner speak his piece.

"Tank treads. Leaving the scene, heading back into the neighborhood."

"I know that footprint," Jake says, more of an accusation than a statement.

The Devastator. Pike.

Mulholland's silence is his affirmation.

***

From the wood-line to the north of the shattered outpost, a sniper rifle lowers. Black Hair watches the huge armored transport growl back down the road as it heads southeast on Fulton Street. He shoulders the big gun and stands, knees and ankles creak as he rises.

He flexes gray fingers, his knuckle bones pop. A hand lined with deep cuts which no longer bleed run over the flap of his dislodged scalp. Strands of ebon hair detach themselves under the action, he simply shakes them off.

A rictus smile shows his dis-colored teeth.

"Captain... Jacob... Billet... must die," he growls, and starts to move through the woods following the Huron.

Chapter Five
Washed Up Dead

"**W**hat do you mean the Major's left the area?"

Light rain peppers Jake's face. It is cooling but can't extinguish the angry words he blasts upon the young corporal who stands inside the Butterworth Test Facility's main entrance barricade.

The grunt swallows hard and stands stoic before Billet and the Huron. "You'll have to speak to Grounds Commander Felder. I know he saw the TC's manifest and signed off departure papers. I understand the rendezvous with him was here, but…"

Billet holds up his hand, cuts the guard short. The corporal steps aside as Jake, grumbling, slogs through the wet, matted grass towards the beige-roofed CO's pavilion.

Loutonia appears in the Huron's commander's hatch, pulls on her olive-colored beret as the rain spatters off her short-shorn dark hair. Stokes busily wraps his quad guns with a small blue tarp as he watches Jake storm off. A guard at a secondary inner perimeter fence opens the gate, lets the agitated man walk through without stopping him.

"You going in there to make sure he doesn't step into a dog pile or something?" Loutonia says to Stokes.

Stokes cinches down the tarp. His hand slips off the moisture-slick bungee cord. He nearly backhands himself in the face.

"Hell, no." He shakes his head. "You won't catch me living, or dead in there."

The Butterworth Test Facility is 180-acres of what was once a landfill superfund site. When the Blight occurred, and the Zombie Trooper Program launched, the grounds made the perfect place for a testing and training facility for the military's undead science sector. It is a place a soldier doesn't want to visit when mortally wounded and their earthly coil begins to fray.

Phelps nods at the gunner. As soldiers, contractually they have signed their life and unlife away. Injected with Datropoline vaccine which protected them during the onset of the virus, it turned out the drug's side effect didn't let a person die naturally.

Loutonia touches one of her .45's holstered at her hip. There is a Smith & Wesson means to remedy the contractual issue.

"I'll tag along behind him," Loutonia climbs out of the hatch and slides over Huron's side.

Stokes watches the woman trot across the soupy roadbed, wrapping her arms about herself against the increasing downpour.

"Heard about the place, but never been here." Campau emerges from the hatch their driver just exited. He scans the tall fence lines, the buildings off in the distance set atop a slight rise. Several groups of literal ragtag troops meander about the enclosed drill grounds.

"It's where good soldiers go when they die," Stokes says, tries to light the stump of cigar as it bounces in the corner of his mouth. He gives up on the smoke, gnaws on the wet butt instead, and pulls the hood of his rain poncho tighter over his head. He slinks low within his own hatch, a snake in a hole.

Knowing the history of the squat gunner, Campau opens his mouth to reply but decides against it. He ducks back down within the dry confines of the Huron.

At the rear gunner's hatch, Eddie Mulholland stands silent in his own port. He shivers as he stares at the compound, though not due to the rain's cool bite.

***

Jake waits as the inner gate opens for him. The trooper on the other side talks into a headset and seems to have trouble contacting the security tower perched atop the main pavilion's rooftop.

"I'm sorry, sir. We had clear channels for a while this morning, and then everything crapped out," the guard says, presses the ear piece to his head, looks at the tower as he does so.

Crapped out so you could do your own dirty work, Billet thinks: Pike, the tank tracks and the destroyed M45 Outpost on his mind. He can't believe the man would cripple a main artery like the outpost. Why Jeremy did it and has the balls to leave a trail makes Jake's head hurt worse.

Is the TC and his crew going AWOL? Is it something with the drug-tracking device Pike had in his possession, something to destroy city property over? Are they buying or dealing outside of town, in cahoots with Reganshire or some other shady entity outside city limits?

None of it makes sense, but Jake knows it is adds up to something. He is sure he won't like when all the pieces fall together.

The tall gate jerks and starts to slowly open, then stops abruptly. The guard swears and puts his hands against the metal framework, pushing.

"The rain's really mucking with our equipment." The guard gnashes his teeth as he pushes without success against the chain link gate.

Billet tries to assist, but quits when his boot heels go ankle deep in the mud.

"I'll call down some assistance," the guard says, gets back on the horn to the tower.

The test facility consists of a series of fence lines. An outer ring lines the entire property while an inner ring protects the main compound buildings. In between the outer and inner ring, like bicycle spokes, gated corridors connect them. The GRCC hates the reference, but people call these spoke areas "pens" where the freshly re-invigorated undead soldiers march and become reacquainted with military life.

Even under the brooding, rain-spitting sky, the ZT's are out doing maneuvers, directed by living Drill Sergeants.

A small training "pen" to Billet's left holds a dozen ZT's. They march with mud-weighted footsteps. Those he can recognize, men and women who still hold enough of a semblance of their former selves, stomp the ground. Gray, sneering faces reveal red gums and clenched teeth. The poor grunts retain all their core military skills, with amped-up very dangerous aggression. It makes Jake's gut churn.

The troops parade by the fence line while holding mock wood weapons.

A ZT peers Jake's way, eyeballs as cloudy as the day.

Billet's head throbs. He blinks, surprised to find the undead trooper stopped and saluting him. The other troops stop, some rear-ending their brother or sister in front of them.

Though only the one seemed to notice him at first, suddenly the entire group turns to face him. Arms raise, some bandaged tight to keep stitched limbs from falling apart. The group salutes him with grumbles and moans against unused or damaged vocal cords.

Captain.

The word is more in his head than from undead tongue.

"Captain? Jake?" Jake turns to find Loutonia beside him. She fists his shoulder painfully. "The gate's open for us," she says.

He turns back to the undead troopers. They stomp down the line like they had been.

They pay him no heed.

"Commander Felder is in Building Two waiting for you,"

the gate guard says as he and two other soldiers stand beside him, wiping the rain from their brow.

"Come on, hun, er... Captain," Loutonia clears her throat and looks sheepishly at the other men who appear to not have heard her. "You look like hell. Let's get you out of the rain."

Jake swallows the sudden lump in his throat as they pass through the last gate.

He throws up.

***

"Don't talk."

The room is painted egg shell white, ceiling stained a dirty yellow by cigarette smoke. Commander Hank Felder stands lean as a fence post within his personal examination room, a Pall Mall between his thin-fleshed skeletal fingers. He looks to have been a jolly man at some time in his life, but the years and his position have obviously taken a toll on him. His clothing fits loosely about his gangly frame and areas of his exposed skin droop. He smiles at Billet, the loose jowl flesh hangs like mottled pink drapery.

Jake pulls the thermometer from his mouth, hands it brusquely to the doctor who stands beside Felder.

"How long have you had these headaches and sensitivity to light?" Felder asks. He eyeballs Jake like a kid who's taken a bad spill off a bike.

Billet groans, then squints as Felder hits the dimmer switch behind him, makes the room glare.

"What the fuck?" Jake shields his eyes. A sharp pain spears through his eyeballs. His brain feels like it's been harpooned with a knitting needle.

Felder dims the lights. Jake slides off the examination table, fists balled.

The doctor steps backwards, reaches for a red button on the wall but does not press it. Yet.

"I didn't come here for a gawddamn physical," Billet says, grits his teeth. "For all we know you got a rogue TC out there with a big ass piece of armament, planning to do God knows what, and you want to check to make sure, what, I'm not turning or something?"

The doctor nods in agreement.

Felder's eyes narrow at the doctor.

The doctor changes his positive nod to a negative shake, and looks at Billet. "Uh… no, nothing like that," he says quickly.

"Captain, please calm down. They're only trying to help." Loutonia stands beside Jake. She places a hand on his and he immediately relaxes his fist.

Felder notices her gesture, nods at the doctor. The doctor pens something on his clipboard.

"I'm not dead yet," Jake returns, though the anger ebbs with the touch of his driver's cool hand on his warm flesh.

"Listen," he continues, "We have a compromised western outpost. Communications are down. Pissed Grand Rapidians and their mayor want their rotting citizens back. For all I know we're going to have to go Noah soon if we get any more rain. And a tank commander and his rig are up to something."

Felder sighs. "You aren't listening to me, Captain." He waits to see if any more words are to pass from the other man. "Major Pike informed us of the situation at the M45 outpost. Due to heavy flooding in some areas the rest of his convoy couldn't manage, they left them behind. He reported his radioman picked up an unknown broadcast from the outpost area and went to investigate. He said they were attacked when they arrived, returned fire, and came straight here as planned and asked us to send the report direct to Central Command once lines were up."

"Must've been one hell of a skirmish." Billet looks towards the lone window in the burnt tobacco-scented room.

Felder's cigarette smoke curls around Jake's head and makes his stomach churn. He realizes he is probably weak and woozy from not eating anything in a while.

The scene outside the window shows more rain and ZT's doing drills in another enclosure.

"We didn't check the integrity of the outer fence," Jake says, "though it looked to still be hanging by a hinge or two."

Felder nods.

"He didn't say anything about who attacked him?" Jake asks.

"Not specifically. I'd have to go get the report." Felder replies and rubs his chin. His cigarette ashes, the burnt flakes roll down his chest to the floor.

"We ran across some opposition at the Apostolate on Valley and Bridge. A couple pick-up trucks and guys tried to lasso some of the civilians," Loutonia adds. "They didn't appear to carry any major ordinance the size to warrant cannon fire from a tank."

Though it made his brain rattle painfully in his skull, it's Jake's turn to nod. He's sure Phelps could also smell the bullshit in Pike's report.

"Speaking of our beloved UCRA friends, on a more positive note," Felder leads Billet and Phelps from the examination room; the doctor watches Jake the entire time as they walk out. "We dredged up the lost victims you and Pike were sent out to retrieve. Lucky, we got the communiqué on the accident before the lines went garbled again. They washed up almost in our back yard."

Billet abruptly stops in the doorway. "You retrieved them all?"

Felder motions them further into the adjoining office. The room reeks of stale cigarette smoke. It's colored brightly, but stained the same yellow tinge. Four monitors flash along the wall opposite the Grounds Commander's desk, views of various areas of the facility show on the screens.

Felder takes a seat behind the desk and inhales what is left of his cigarette. He mashes the butt out in an ashtray overflowing with other butts and ash.

"They came in near the northeast boat launch. I don't know if the damn things were holding hands or what, but they all washed up in a neat little pile." Felder digs a crumpled cigarette pack from his shirt pocket, fingers out a half-bent smoke, lights it up. "The rotted face twins and the couple were so water-logged we had to tip them on end until they drained out." He puffs on the fresh cigarette. "Nothing worse than the soup that comes out of a Zee's gut.

"The big fellow was a bear to haul. We'd been ready with poles and rope, but it took six of my men to secure the brute." Felder inhales again, exhales. No smoke comes out.

Billet can see yesterday's events, the Rhino zomb moving through the troops on the flooded river bank, swatting them aside like empty paper cups.

"We tarped up that boy good compared to the others. Couple yards of tow strap, cinched at head and feet. That one's gonna be a bitch if it gets out of *that* bundle. The others were pretty docile, probably spent all their energy swimming," Felder says. Someone knocks at the office door. "We strapped them on good to the Major's tank. Reminded me of deer hunting in Northern Michigan. Those were the days." Felder stares a million miles away to some distant memory as he takes another deep drag.

Billet has to catch his breath. "Wait a minute. What—"

A soldier drenched from head to toe opens the door and steps into the office. Surprised at the others in the room, he nods his salutations. He salutes Billet, nearly pokes his eye with the missive he pulls from his dripping satchel pack. He slips it across the Grounds CO's desk.

Felder puts a nicotine-stained finger up to ward off further words from Jake. He unfolds and reads the document. Eyes roam the page from left to right. His brow knits and forehead creases the deeper he goes.

"Not good. Not good at all." Felder folds the note and puts it aside. He looks up at the trooper who waits for his next command.

"That'll be all, Lieutenant. Tell Doctor Rutowski I'll be over to see him in a few minutes."

The lieutenant salutes, spins on heel, and leaves the office.

"Not good at all," Felder repeats.

Jake chomps at the bit for more information on Pike's activities and the UCRA citizens. He tries to keep his agitation in check, fails, and says with heated irritation in his voice: "What is it?"

Felder glances up at Billet without moving his head.

Phelps can see the CO is pissed and squeezes Jake's shoulder so he checks himself before they get thrown out.

"We had one of our chemists go AWOL a few days ago. A new prize, fresh young fellow, highly intelligent, though I think he knocked himself down a peg in that category, decided to slip out in the height of the storm and flooding…not very smart," Felder says. He inhales sharply, and exhales in a rattling breath to calm himself.

He simmers down before Billet does.

Too bad about your luck, Jake wants to say, but Loutonia's painful pinch of his shoulder stays his tongue. She knows him all too well.

"The citizens we were slated to find and bring back. Pike's got them?"

"Well, yes," Felder says matter-of-fact, "Your orders were to retrieve and bring them back, right? Pike said once he got the sixth one he'd turn around and head back to the city. He said you could wait here, or head back to town yourself if you so desired.

"I'm not wishing to be in his goulashes, from here to Grandville you've got to wade through a lot of water. Once you get outside the enclosure, about a mile down the road, there's an easy four feet or more of water over Butterworth. The gravel pits and the old Georgia-Pacific plant are lakes currently, though wouldn't want to try fishing. Some Feral activity but not like on a good day. Guess the rain bothers them as much as our tottering civvies."

Butterworth Street runs from the south side of downtown. It

starts on the west side of the Grand River, cuts through the UCRA enclosure, and goes all the way to Wilson Avenue on the village boundary lines of Grandville and Wyoming. From the west side, once beyond the Butterworth/I-196 underpass gate, the road heads out into the boonies. Hilly and tree-lined, the only flat open areas are old gravel and gypsum quarries. Besides rusted hulks of diggers and dump trucks, a few ramshackle houses and the old plasterboard manufacturing plant are the only signs anyone had set foot in the area.

It is also Reganshire's back door as Butterworth connects with Wilson Avenue, and several miles north, Wilson runs to the southern gate of Silas Regan's growing town and fortification.

"You said Pike set out to find the sixth victim?" Jake says, glances at Loutonia. Her perplexed look mimics his thoughts.

"Yes, since communications to the Wilson Bridge Outpost are down, he figured they'd go out that way and see if they netted the sixth one. It's going to be floating or dragging across river bottom by that point," Felder says.

Jake reaches across and shakes the CO's hand; it's like grasping a handful of dry twigs. "We'll be on our way. I don't want the Major and his crew to be outside on their own," he says and winces as his temples suddenly pulse with pain.

Felder nods his agreement. "My doctor can give you something for the headache."

Billet pulls his soggy beret from his waist belt, places it slightly canted on his head. The cool wetness is almost soothing.

"I'll pass," he says, eyes cast for a moment at the video monitors and the view of the undead troopers at drill. "My driver here is our onboard medic. She'll give me the boost."

Hurrying through the complex and heading back out into the rain, Jake looks over his shoulder at Loutonia who follows close behind. "Something's up with our good friend Jeremy Pike."

The rain comes down in a light drizzle, but the dark clouds

above promise a heavier mix again.

"Sixth victim," Loutonia shakes her head, bewildered, "There is no sixth victim, is there?"

"No, and there's reason to trek outside Grand Rapids city limits, no reason to haul those citizens along with him," Billet replies. He looks through the chain link gates they near which will bring them to the Huron. He hopes the big rig can remain water tight for the pursuit, or they might become flood victims themselves.

***

A ZT stops as he watches a man and a woman run by. He recognizes the man, a soldier, the face. He remembers. He bellows, an anguish-filled cry, but it is drowned under a blanket of thunder. The undead soldier grabs at the enclosure with graying fingers and presses his ragged claw-striped face against the chain link.

"Cak-tin, you prom-missed. Prom-missed!" the trooper calls out but his tongue won't wag and vocal cords strum like frayed guitar strings. Nothing works.

He shakes the fence, the entire span precariously rattles. Upon his wet uniform, above the left breast pocket, a name tape stitched with black letters: WILLS.

***

"You got it?" Stokes says to Campau. He holds Huron's navigator by the belt of a spare seat harness.

"I got it," Campau replies, tries to right his helmet with his arm as he leans out over the front of the Huron with a hook pole firmly in hands.

"Don't fall in. It looks deep down there." Stokes says, with a snort of mirth. "And hopefully what's in that body bag isn't still alive."

"Don't fuck with me, man," Colter shoots back, prods the tarped form floating in the water below. He probes with the hook, once, then again, until he jabs, pulls and snags a patch of fabric.

The Huron stands perched on the lip of the very deep puddle. The pool of water crosses a low spot in Butterworth Street. Rain drops dapple the water's surface. A stain of oil is disturbed and its dark rainbow-colored sheen ripples upon the flooded roadway.

Four forms wrapped in blue tarps bob in the oil and mud fogged water.

Billet and Phelps stand on the roadside beside the transport and watch the retrieval activity.

With his boot tips within an inch of the gentle lap of dark water, Jake glances up at his crew. "See anything?" he says to Mulholland who stands on Overwatch, peering through the rain for trouble, assault rifle in hand.

The lanky gunner makes eye contact but looks away when Jake makes direct eye contact with him.

Kid's been acting kooky since we returned from the Lettner mission, Jake thinks. *When this shit job is over it's time to have a talk with him. See what's eating at him.*

"Fuck," Jake moans, "The shit's wearing off already." He feels sick to his stomach. His temples pound all the way to his belly. Each throb is a punch to the gut followed by an upswing, a squeezing tightness in his chest. It makes his breath come up short, feels like a phantom fist grips his heart.

Phelps turns to regard him. "What was that?"

"Nothing," he says quickly, fights a sudden bout of dizziness he hopes she doesn't notice. "Just sick… of the rain." She had given him a medicinal stim shot before they left the BTF. *Twenty minutes ago. System must be building up a tolerance.*

With the tarp firmly hooked, Campau directs it to where Billet and Phelps stand. Jake pulls his sidearm as Phelps withdraws one of her .45's, ready for anything. He notices a puckered black hole where the head of the body within the heavy cloth wrap is located.

"Looks like someone did the job for us," Loutonia says, holsters her gun and gives the bundle a rough prod with her boot.

The thing inside the body bag is totally and, for certain, dead.

Jake keeps pistol in hand. He watches as Lou squats and peels open the wet tarp. He surprises himself as a wave of nausea threatens to make him lose his guts all over his driver's back side. Instead, he gulps down the knot of bile and grimaces when the gift within the tarp is revealed.

"That is one ugly SOB." Loutonia puts her sleeve to her face, tries to block the stench.

Billet takes a look at the dead-dead Zee. "One of the twins. Its' brother is one of those," he motions towards the remaining floaters, "and the undead couple will be in the mix too."

Jake glances across the flooded roadway where the asphalt reappears some twenty yards away. He can't see Pike but he knows he and the Devastator are out there.

"Shot them and dumped them, and kept the big one. What the hell?" Loutonia huffs.

Campau prods another tarp bundle, pokes it like he's trying to harpoon a chunk of steak with a fork.

"He seems to like that big one," she says placing the tarp back over the gruesome face of the dead Zee.

A second body is slid up beside the first. Inner ailments gone for the moment, Jake leans down and unveil this one. He winces as his brain bangs against his forehead.

The second body is in fact the female of the couple who'd gone in the drink. A puckered black hole the size of a dime shows above her left eye. She wears an almost relieved expression upon her gray face.

Billet feels envious of her final state, fully departed from the crazy world they live upon.

"There's gonna be some very pissed off folk back in town. Pike's going to further fuck up the relationship between us and the Townies." Loutonia says, watches Campau wrestle with the third body as it bobs like a cork eluding capture.

Jake wants to chuckle at her new name for the Grand Rapids folk they protect and die for, but the few words prior poke him harder than their navigator's sloppy spear fishing.

"Pike doesn't give a shit. He's working on his own agenda." Jake again looks down the road. "The big one has something Pike wants, or has to have.

"I don't think I told you but right before the scuffle on the river bank, Pike had one of those handheld tracking devices the druggies use to find their substance of choice, said he'd been tasked to track an illegal shipment of Datropoline being carried by one of the UCRA civilians."

Billet is interrupted as Campau swears, sees Stokes lose his grip on the other man's harness. The navigator's helmet cants sideways and drops into the drink with a splash as Stokes reaffirms his grip. The helmet sinks out of sight.

Loutonia frowns at the lost gear. Jake shrugs, it'd come out of the kid's pay.

"Pike went ape shit when the big guy busted out and went in the river. I never saw anyone sign up so fast to head back out in this shit."

The third body gets slid up to Billet's boot tips. He lets Loutonia take this one. She sucks in a breath and unwraps the head section. It is the male counterpart of the married couple; with a perforated cranium like his bride.

"So, what do you think he's up to?" Loutonia says as she drags the body further out of the water so it doesn't set sail again.

Jake watches Campau snag and push the last body towards them.

"You hit the nail on the head when you said he is dumping

them. He's dumping and running, unloading what he doesn't need to carry. He knows he'd end up getting an ass load of heat from Command and everyone else if he went back home…"

The sky rumbles overhead.

"He doesn't care because he's got other plans," though Jake can't quite put his finger on what Jeremy's plans might be.

"Still doesn't explain what he's up to. How much does black market Datropoline bring in? What would anyone want with that stuff?" Loutonia says.

Billet shivers at the thought. Rebecca Regan comes to mind.

"Some think it's a ticket to immortality…if you like to walk with the dead."

"Or you could make your own batch of undead troopers. Inject some trained pukes like us, do all but put a bullet in their brain so they're like the poor bastards at the BTF…" She latches onto the last tarp-wrapped body. "…and you got yourself the start of a small army."

A light bulb flares in Jake's mind. He winces under its painfully bright revelation.

"Place the bodies far enough inland so they don't slip back into the water. We'll pick them up on the way back," Billet waves his fist in the downpour to keep his crew's attention. He looks again at the waist deep flooded road and off into the distance, he envisions the potential course of the Pike and the Rhino.

Reganshire. Reganshire is the nearest town once out of this wet quarry and wooded countryside.

Stokes and Campau come down and assist with pulling the bodies up to a section of roadway that should be safe from the rising water. The navigator crumbles expletives at the sergeant, still miffed over the loss of his helmet. Stokes smiles.

"That'll do," Jake says as he stands upright after dragging one of the twins. The bodies should be far enough from any threat of making contact with the flooding. No one drives Butterworth except military vehicles—or people who shouldn't.

He looks back in the direction they have traveled then up into the woods. If any Ferals are about they might tear into the free bagged meals. Not his problem at this point. There is bigger game to bag.

Jake clambers back aboard the Huron, steps upon the rooftop. He slip, catches himself on the hatch ring of his own cupola. He shakes off a bout of dizziness, fights his gut trying to tornado up his throat. "Load up." He pumps his fist, hopes if his crew notices him fumble they'd see he has steadied himself. "We got a tank to catch."

Feel like shit. Feel way like shit. Jesus not now.

He pours himself into the commander's hatch, drops into the belly of the Huron and discharges on the steel grating what is left in his stomach.

***

The scope tips up. Black Hair wipes the lens with a wet sleeve. It does little to remove the moisture on the gun sight.

Re-acquiring the target, he sees it slip into the protective steel shell of the big transport.

He growls in frustration. A crimson vision: a dead transport commander with a bullet-shattered skull. Blood. Brains. Meat.

The flame of frustration blows out as a grisly smile splits Black's gray jowls. In the red flare of thought, he sees himself bent over the corpse, gnawing, tearing, feasting upon the brain soup within the destroyed cranial bowl.

He shoulders the rifle, peers up into the crying sky. He cannot feel the cool rain drops upon his dead flesh, but he smiles all the same.

It is just a matter of time before dinner is served.

Chapter Six
Dead Lines

"You still alive?"

Phelps' cool hands run across Jake's scar-lined face as she speaks close to his ear. The soothing touch makes him want to hunker down against her, feel her against him; let himself fall into her embrace for eternity.

The Huron rumbles, moving.

She wipes a damp cloth about his neck, brings it up from the water swirling around their boots. He doesn't flinch, hardly feels it, as she jabs him, injects him with another dose of pain-relieving medicine. The fever, the feeling of bursting into flames, subsides. His heartbeat slows, returns to normal; no more of the irregular, breath stealing thump-skip-thump.

"I think you're getting worse." Loutonia helps him into one of the interior seat pans. "Are you sure you don't want us to turn around and go back to the test facility, or maybe head back to town? I have one medi-pak left. If you or anyone else need it..."

"No," Jake says through grit teeth. He fights to control the sudden red flash of anger in his head. "I'm fine. Just... under the weather. When we get back, then I'll see a doctor, not anyone from the BTF. Ever."

He looks into Loutonia's brown eyes. "You put a bullet in my brain before you bring me in *there* for a cure."

She falls into him, wraps arms around him. They do not share their intimacy under public scrutiny though it is well known to the other crew members they are together, lovers. He does not push her away to remind her of the proper place for such affections, but it feels good; feels good to be in the embrace. He doesn't care about the flash of dizziness which twists and twirls his mind.

Lou holds him tight. He couldn't break her grip if he tried. And he doesn't want to.

"Don't worry. I'll be fine." Jake gives her a small squeeze to let her know he's regained his calm.

She holds on for a moment longer, and then releases him. He can see the worry in her eyes. He is thankful for having someone again in his life, caring about him as such.

There'd been a time after his wife and son died where he felt maybe that was it for him. He never expected he'd find himself in another relationship; and with his driver no less; a hard-ass woman and soldier who'd as soon kick a man's balls into his brain case for looking at her sideways. She'd lost something greater than herself as he, and in that they shared a common bond: the loss of spouse and children.

"Someone's got to watch over you," she says as she draws in close and presses her lips to his. She rears back in the same instant. "God, you're cold."

"Now that's not nice to say." He pulls her back into him. Maybe she can't feel it, but he can. He can feel her warmth; practically hear her blood pumping strong through her veins. He can smell her heat.

He feels the cool water on the Huron's floor soak into the seams of his combat boots. It draws him out of the kiss.

He turns to see Mulholland squatting in his cupola. Jake looks his way and Eddie bolts upright, as if he didn't want them to know he'd been watching. His head hits the side of the turret strut, mashes his helmet down hard against his skull. The gunner winces, rights his head gear and slowly resumes his crouch.

"We're about through the thick of it, sir," Mulholland says, nods towards the two-inches of water covering the interior floor. The water slaps against the few wooden crates left in the rear of the transport. "We've seen a couple FZ's out there. They won't be bothering anyone anymore. The Devastator's leaving a nice trail."

"So much for Felder's reconnaissance report," Billet grabs his helmet and starts to rise. "Let's stay frosty. If the wild dog zombs react to the weather like our friendly neighborhood Zees, they'll be ten times more apt to tussle with us."

Loutonia places a hand on Jake's shoulder to stop further ascent.

"What?" Jake says to her.

Mulholland rises—avoids the head butt to metal this time—and takes his station again.

"You're in no condition to go topside. Stay down here. Rest. No sense in you catching pneumonia on top of whatever else ails you."

The Huron lurches to a stop, sends a small wave of water racing forward then back to the rear of the vehicle.

"I'm going to have fun scrubbing this mess out," Loutonia grumbles.

Campau, in the driver's seat, leans his head through the cab doorway. "Believe it or not, I've picked up some long range frequency radio chatter. Garbled, but something," he says. "And there's a light show and thunder in the distance, and it isn't the incoming storm."

Machine gun fire and 120mm cannon fire. No incoming storm? "Or maybe it is," Jake growls, secures his helmet as he rises into his commander's hatch. He ignores Loutonia's squally look.

Her frustration with him is one storm he knows he can

weather, compared to what he suspects will come when they drive into the storm down the road.

***

Gun fire. The hell storm is, in fact, coming from the ground, not from the brooding sky.

The roar of the Devastator's main gun causes a fiery flash of ground lightning. Machine gun fire sends soft rapid *pop* noises in the distance.

Billet estimates it's coming from the old gypsum processing plant three-quarter miles down the road. The low, dark cloud cover bounces the sounds of battle close to the ground and flares its light show above the tree tops.

"They've run into something," Jake says, tilts his helmet down so only the lower part of his face takes the rain.

"Only thing over there besides the wallboard plant is that broadcasting tower," Campau comments over the vehicle commlink.

The bark of a .30-cal behind him, twists Billet around with a start. Mulholland fires behind him and across Huron's roof. All Jake sees is a red vapor as a Feral Zee becomes two as its head flies under the biting assault and deadly accuracy of the gunner's machine gun fire.

"The FZ's got radio intelligence now?" Stokes turns his own quad guns towards the north, off road, and points towards a large man-made flat scrape of land—one of several old sand and gravel quarries in the area.

Surprised to see the 25mm cannon and single TOW missile canister pivot northward following Stokes movement, Billet yells over the discharge of the front gunner's quad machine guns: "Get that damn r/c helmet off!"

The Huron slams to a halt, jerks Jake's midsection painfully into the hatch coaming. A hodge-podge of angry chatter breaks across his helmet's headphones as Phelps lays into Campau, screeches at him for handing off the gun turret controls to Stokes.

The gravel pit to the north holds a combination of sandy mounds and scalloped grassy knolls. The front two-thirds of the quarry sit lower than the roadbed; currently more a shallow lake dotted with various sized islands. A large berm of sand and rock, with an ancient Safety Orange porta-john, stands left of center. On the island, a dozen Feral Zees run upright, some on all fours, back and forth along the front edge of the sand pile, excited at the sight and scent of the massive military can of meat parked roadside.

"Save the ammo. They aren't fond of the water," Billet commands even as both his gunners jerk their guns towards a lone rotter galloping through a shallow pool a few yards away.

Mulholland blows its head off before Stokes can squeeze the trigger.

Stokes flips off his gunner compatriot.

Mulholland returns the gesture and immediately swings his single barrel down and around, throws hot lead in the disfigured face of a second Feral coming out of the bushes on the other side of the transport.

"You kids get it in line and get this tin can rolling," Billet says at the bickering driver and navigator. He draws his sidearm, looks over his side of the vehicle. He doesn't want anything jumping out and up on his side.

"Watch this, Alabama Boy."

"Stokes!" Jake bellows.

The 25mm gun burps loudly three times.

A plume of dirt and smoke erupts on the front right edge of the large Zee-infested island followed by a direct hit on the orange porta-john. Shards of plastic and other questionable detritus fly in all directions. Ferals too close to the outdoor lavatory are bowled over by the first two shots. The third shot geysers the water behind the island, throwing a shower of mud onto a few rotters standing in the rear.

"Good golly," Mulholland exaggerates his natural southern accent to expound upon Stoke's "Alabama-Boy" remark. "You done kilt that toilet but good."

Billet's rising growl extinguishes further exchange between the two gunners.

"Goddamnit, when I give a fucking command, soldier, you fucking listen," Jake goes off like an atomic bomb, all reason and rational washed away. Blood red is his sight; anger absolute with an all-consuming need to lash out.

Stokes jaw hangs open and he peers wide-eyed at Billet. The sergeant stares at M11 SIG Sauer pistol Jake points point-blank in his face.

Billet trembles, teeth clenched. One part of his mind screams at him to not pull the trigger, to lower the pistol. The angry red haze flooding his brain rushes forward, overwhelms the other thought.

Kill the little insubordinate motherfucker!

Jake's finger slowly draws back on the trigger.

"Jacob." A voice. Female. Soft. Jenna's. His dead wife.

"What?" The words terse, yet he eases finger off the trigger.

He feels a hand on his lower leg.

"Jake," Loutonia's voice sounds from below.

The red haze falls like loosened drapery.

"Is everything all right up there…Captain?" she asks.

He lowers the gun, trigger finger off trigger and on the trigger guard. He shows Stokes there's no longer a threat.

"I'm sorry. I'm… not feeling well." The rain on Jake's face hisses from the heat of his shame and embarrassment. "When we're done here…"

"It's fine, Cap. I know. I know. I should've been listening."

The gunner pulls the transmission plug from the input on the side of the r/c helmet, severs the link between it and the cannon turret. Under the rim of his own stand, he holsters his own sidearm partially withdrawn from its hard leather holster.

Billet nods and turns ahead, ignores the Ferals stranded on the little island of sand as they swarm upon the smoking wreckage of their porta-john fazed partners. "Keep moving. We've already let our friends ahead know we're here."

Stokes returns to his quad guns.

Thankful no one notices, Mulholland quickly spins the barrel of his 30-Cal away from the commander's hatch, taking the gun bead off his captain's forehead.

***

The Georgia-Pacific gypsum board plant sits on 80-acres of land, the earth flattened to calm the rolling hills of the area and let the manufacturing building sprawl amidst the surrounding woodland. The wallboard plant had shut down in the mid 1990's. The building and land had gone up for sale without success. The entire place had fallen into disrepair. The concrete drives and parking lots overtaken by weeds and tall grasses, even a smattering of sparse-limbed shrubs. A small mountain of scrap wallboard rose on the properties back lot waited to be reclaimed by time and the elements.

The Huron rolls at half-speed through the already fallen and crumpled fence and gate. Jake secures his own Caliber-30 to his hatch ring and gives the green light to limited actions with the 25mm gun. Still feeling the sting from the ball out several minutes ago, Stokes keeps the turret gear off and keeps hands on his familiar quad guns. Mulholland watches their backs in case any further Ferals feel interested in popping out of the soggy underbrush.

Across the property, on the opposite side of the building, small arms and machine gun fire fill the air along with the pine of the Devastator's turbine engines.

"If they weren't so intent on studying the effects of all the rot-on-legs, the EPA would have a field day with this place," Campau says as Loutonia slows the rig further and creeps along the facility's east face.

The side of the building ramps skyward, a wall of collapsed and curved steel and aluminum reveal shadowy innards. The wallboard fabrication machinery—presses, massive rollers and conveyor systems—look like huge fallen beasts that have died and decayed. Twisted skeletal remains stand forever silent and captured inside. Exposed steel ribs and rusted vertical I-beams paint the ground red. A faded yellow bulldozer, sagging and dilapidated as the building, shows an engine which has bled out and soaks the soil an oily brown-black; the area around it bare except for the crumpled grasses and weeds trying to grow, and failing, in the polluted ground.

Two men rush from the remains of an open doorway. They brandish semi-automatic rifles. They skid to a halt on the muddy ground.

"Hold your fire," Billet says, his hands on his gun grips.

Stokes swivels around. "Friendlies?"

Dressed in civilian garb, both men lift their weapons and open fire.

Bullets ping off the face of the Huron.

One of the men goes to his belt line, lifts his arm and tosses an olive-colored ball. The ball, a grenade, lands several feet in front of the transport. It explodes in a curl of flame and mud.

Jake looks sideways at Stokes, "With main guns only..." Billet nods. "Light them up."

The ground blooms red where the two attackers had stood.

"Captain, we have a lot of radio chatter. Jamming frequency must've fell away," Campau says over the comm.

"Open all channels."

Jake breathes out, a moment of relief, as Campau switches to the broader channels they had been unable to utilize most of the trip. His helmet's headphones erupt into a world of voices all talking at the same time.

"...back online. Calling all GRCC outriders. Please report in."

"…need immediate support if any units in locale. Repeat. Butterworth Test Facility populace destabilized. Please assist if you're receiving…"

"…ganshire amassing new vehicles and recruits. We think they may be preparing for…"

"…cut the broadcast. Cut the broadcast. If they trace this back to…"

From the opposite side of the building, the Devastator's main gun roars. Over the sound of small arms fire, tortured metal shrieks.

"Holy shit," Mulholland says as he, Jake and Stokes glance skyward.

Looming like a slender skeletal cone, the usurped broadcast tower in the rear of the building shudders then slowly bends forward. Antennae wave and droop. Bundles of radio and satellite dishes shake free and trail thin veins of wire behind them.

"Phelps, full reverse. Now!" Billet yells, his breath catches in his chest as he watches the 150-foot broadcast tower—rivets shearing, steel cross-members snapping, cables loose and lashing—fall towards them.

Gears grind. It takes a long breath to halt the massive transport, and another to start its roll rearwards.

Billet white-knuckles the hatch ring, his eyes on the tower's descent.

With a heavy tinny chime of tortured metal, the tower crashes to the ground, splits the muddy two-track the Huron recently traversed.

"You can thank your loyal City Treasurer Rupert Largo," Pike's voice suddenly booms over the comm.

With the jamming broadcast and tower destroyed, the broader channels are squelched with the hills and trees creating more interference. However, the short wave broadcast is solid, and Pike knows the internal channel Huron relies. The communication between vehicles is clear as if Pike stands inside the big HTV.

"What's the Sitrep, Major?" Billet asks. He strains to keep from losing it and blasting the man with a string of expletives. "You almost dropped that transmission tower on our head."

Phelps brings the Huron around 180 degrees, heads back the way they came in. A paved roadbed circles around the front of the building. Jake hears the report of more rifle and machine gun fire, including the hiss and dull explosive impact of what Billet assumes is a rocket-propelled grenade. The turbine whine of the Abrams, and report of its own machine guns, informs him the battle on the other side of the old plant isn't over.

"Loyalists of your old pal Lettner and our dear Mr. Largo," Pike replies, a bit of static clips the broadcast as the tanks' machine guns bark. "You can cut the head off the dog, but the fleas will still roam."

Billet can see the battle is mainly man against machine as the Huron churns around to the building's west side. He counts roughly a dozen men hunkered down near the rear of the old factory and the concrete footings of the collapsed radio tower. A dozen more lay in mostly indiscernible bloody piles between building, tower and tank.

Pike and crew are buttoned up inside the Devastator. They take no chances. Two spots on the turret and one on the left side skirting bear marks where rocket-propelled grenade have struck, like someone splashed a bucket of smoky black paint on the impact points. The shots did no real damage to the 120mm thick armor of the 68 ton Devastator.

Jake has no real concern of serious vehicular damage to the Huron by small weapons fire, even a RPG hit. They can limp along with a blown tire; a damaged track can be repaired; a gun mount, dinged hatch, headlamp or antenna can be fixed. Damage to person is another subject, but none of them will back down if someone throws lead at them or their machine.

"Mulholland, eyes left. Stokes, right."

A man leans around a doorway near the rear of the building. He squeezes off two rounds from his rifle and ducks back behind the sheet metal door as one shot rings off the Huron's hull.

Jake lights up the closed portal, shell casings bounce off the Huron's iron hide as his Cal.-30 blazes. Lead pounds into the door so hard it falls from its rusted hinges. Perforated by bullets up, down and sideways, the aperture now qualifies as a screen door. Underneath the fixture, the rifleman is forever still, his blood the movement as it drools down the blasted doorframe and wall.

The brethren of the downed man let loose with their own salvo.

"Jesus, man. Remind me not to get on your bad side," Stokes says over the four barrel crack of his own .30's.

Billet doesn't respond as Loutonio turns the Huron at an angle so all three topside guns can fire without overlap. His machine gun has little recoil, snug in its mount as it is, but every prolonged burst rattles his arms, hammers at his brain. His gut does a flip flop, sends a lump of something up into his throat. He feels he is going to be sick again and stops firing and lets his gunners do their job.

Jake slides down into the cradle of his commander's stand: "I know there's some Lettner folk out and about causing trouble. But what are these accusations about Largo? I know the guy's as slippery as an eel, but you can't tell me Lettner and he were in cahoots." He hopes Pike is still dialed in. He doesn't care if their crews listen.

"You've been on the road too long, playing up to your big ex-father-in-law in Muskegon and being the hero," Pike chimes in. "Assisting the lakeshore commonwealth and Grand Rapids, the precious hub of West Michigan."

Jake's anger grows hot with the comment about the current NSC Muskegon commissioner, his father-in-law, still, even though the man's daughter, his wife, is dead. Jeremy can't let it go, can't stop chiding him over the mission the TC hadn't been picked for.

"Since you took the prior NSC trash out," Jeremy adds as if

he replies to Jake's thoughts, "You've been out of sync with things."

More than you know, Jake thinks, his head pounding.

Dulled by the muddy ground, an explosion shakes the Huron.

"Get the rotten grenade-spittin' bastard," Stokes yells over the comm and from above.

"He's in my sights," Mulholland reports.

"No, I got him." Stokes says.

"His buddy's handing him a fresh one."

"Keep him from hitting my rig," Loutonia breaks in.

"I got him." Stokes repeats.

Billet hears two short sharp shots ring out from the Huron's rear.

"You asshole. I said I had them," finishes Stokes.

Bullets continue to ping like hail stones off the Huron's hull.

Pike continues as if he and Billet sit in easy chairs sharing a beer and simple conversation: "Lettner and Largo are cut from the same cloth when it comes to beliefs. They want to see eradication of all the undead populace, and perhaps a few living obstacles," Jeremy says over the drum of his own machine gunner lancing into the men in the field, "It's just that Largo hasn't made the step up to where he really wants to be."

Jake feels what Pike says almost impossible to grasp. What reason would Largo have for interfering with communications from the city? It isn't a way to gain popularity if caught. Billet knows Largo is after Honeywell's job, but doing something on the cusp of a terrorist act. It doesn't make sense.

"We're getting off subject," Billet says. "You've been by the M45 Outpost. Explain. And putting a bullet in those undead civvies, and wrapping that big sonofabitch and feeding the BTF a line of bull about a sixth?"

There is silence on Pike's end. For a moment Billet isn't sure if the TC hesitates so he can make up another bullshit excuse, or the man simply isn't going to answer.

"Enemy neutralized," Stokes says over the comm. "Do you want us to check the casualties?"

Billet reaches over and raps on the 25mm turret column. Stokes ducks down to meet him.

"Stay put. I need to make sure they're all neutralized," Jake says.

Stokes gives him a queer look.

Jake ignores it and sits back down in his hatch seat.

"You aren't answering me, Major," he continues.

"I don't think I like your tone," Pike responds with irritation. "What are you implying, Captain?" He paints the last word boldly, emphasizing the distinction between their ranks.

"We have a shell-blasted outpost with your track marks at the scene, a lie to a field officer at the BTF, a group of shot up UCRA civilians by your hand or orders, and a big ass Zee with contraband inside it. And you continue to head south," Billet snarls. His head hurts and the arm he uses to lean against the hatch stoop feels weighted. He will be damned though if Pike's going to get away with what Jake's certain the man is in the act of doing.

"Jacob...?" Loutonia leans out of her seat, half in the cab archway. "Jesus, what are you doing?"

He ignores her and slowly climbs back topside.

The sky is still chalk gray, only a drop or two of rain hits his face. Off towards the wallboard factory, the ground lay disheveled, chewed and thrown in chunks from the gun fire. The bodies of the Loyalists, or whoever they might be, stretch across the silent battlefield, torn and red.

A squelch of static breaks across the commlink, and broken garbled voices are heard in and out of the hiss and pop.

"Campau, make a call to Command. Tell them what's going on. Everything." Billet says.

"Umm...but what exactly *is* going on?" Campau replies.

The channel is still open between the Huron and Devastator.

"That's my question also," Pike, in everyone's headset.

Diesel turbines rev and whine. The tank turret swivels, the 120mm main gun points at the Huron.

Jake sees they are the Devastator's target.

Oh shit.

"The outpost was destroyed by the time we got there. We chased a couple curious rotters away from the enclosure with small arms fire, that was it," Jeremy growls, murderous annoyance in his voice. "I would've called it in, but obviously could not. Felder told you, didn't he? Everything else is… classified."

Jake doesn't know what to believe, and barely registers anyone else talking at him as he looks at the big gun. The Huron has thick skin but not enough to stop a HEAT round from the Devastator, not from afar, definitely not at close range.

"Son of a bitch just made a new enemy," Stokes says lowly. His hand raises to the r/c gun helmet still affixed atop his head; hairy-knuckled index finger slowly flexes outward to turn the relay switch back on.

"Don't do it," Mulholland, quickly, panicky, takes the words out of Billet's opening mouth.

Campau sees the tank's position, rouses Phelps.

"Umm, Captain? Orders?" Loutonia's voice pinched, tense.

Billet's silence is the command.

"I hear nothing from you now, Jacob. What gives?" Pike taunts.

Jake fights to keep himself in check as a sudden flush of volcanic anger threatens to burst from him. He has never felt such seething rage. His entire body shakes. He starts to raise his hand to make the call: pour everything the Huron has into the tank.

But he isn't suicidal, and he isn't sure the Major bluffs with his main gun thrust in their face.

He lowers his hand. His actions speak louder than words, and in Jake's pounding heart he realizes what really hurts.

Considering their rocky relationship, one of intense

competition and current squabbles, Jake has always known respect for the man: Jeremy Pike. They are cut closer out of the same cloth than either of them want to attest: passionate about the same thing; passionate about their military roles, their sense of duty.

That is why, inside, it kills Billet, kills him to know the GRCC is losing a good man.

Pike's crew is not a wet-behind-the-ears bunch. Davison, McGraw, Larsen—they'll be missed.

And with them, the Devastator, the GRCC's biggest and baddest main battle tank of their dwindling fleet.

Colonel Jackson is going to go nuclear when he finds out Pike and crew has bugged out, gone AWOL.

"I'm sorry to leave you with the undead baggage. I had no means to feed those citizens and I'm going have enough trouble with this big one I'm carrying," Pike says as the Devastator's twin turbines wind up.

"I have Z-rations you know. I can take that one off your hands," Billet, his one last test for the TC. *Take it! Take it and let's not go this route.*

Again, there is hesitation on the other end of the line. Jake can hear a muffled conversation, Pike's voice stands out but he can't hear what is being said.

The line goes completely silent.

And then...

"I told you, Jacob, this is my mission. Final perhaps." Pike says, softer. But it is only for that brief moment, then, his voice rises again in a fierce, threatening tenor. "Don't follow us. Don't try to stop us, or I'll bury you and your crew in that steel box you call a war machine."

The Devastator, with its front end facing southwest and main gun still squarely pointed at the Huron, begins to roll forward and away.

"And watch your back with Largo. Watch your back," are the

TC's final words as the big tank starts up the hillside towards the road.

"What? We're just going to let them get away?" Stokes barks, turns from Jake to the departing tank, and back again. "They're jumping ship, running whatever that big zomb is carrying inside it. We're just going to sit here and watch them leave?"

Jake's heart pounds like the Devastator's main gun blasting inside his head. He closes his eyes, grits his teeth. He tries to fight back the pain as each slam in his chest sends a jolt to his head, sledgehammer hard. He grips the hatch coaming, knuckles white with strain. He turns away so his front gunner can't see his battle, and takes several deep breaths until the throbbing lessens enough so he can speak. Still, when he opens his eyes, for a second, the world cants sideways and he has to catch himself though he isn't falling.

"Campau, can you get a clear, secure channel back to HQ?" he asks, flexes his fingers against the hatchway's cool metal skin.

"Already on it, sir."

"Tell them..." Jake hesitates. He watches the Devastator crawl up the hill towards the main road. He watches it crest the top, main gun traversing back into a forward facing position as the tank grinds over the roadside embankment.

He looks at Stokes who stands and tries to light a fresh stogie. The man fumes with such fervor he can hardly hold the lit match.

"Tell them we're going tank hunting."

Stokes drops the lit match on himself, and then pats himself out though his damp garments would have never flamed up.

Mulholland moans loudly from the rear of the transport.

"It's suicide," Loutonia says over the comm.

Again, Billet's anger flares. A red haze drifts over his eyesight. Heart pounds. Head throbs. He flexes his fingers; his left hand tingles with pin pricks.

"Get this machine going," he snarls. "We'll see who buries who."

Chapter Seven
Death Metal

With M4A1 rifle in hand, Mulholland runs along the pine row on the north side of Butterworth. He keeps low, blends with the rain-dappled rocks, bramble and tall grasses in the shadows of both dreary day and tree.

On one side, making its way at a leisurely pace, thinking all is clear and they've won their freedom, the Devastator growls down the roadway.

Running parallel and a little behind, on the opposite side of the tree-limned bank, the Huron keeps pace, treads through another tract of land: a massive sand quarry.

"They're still hold up inside. Pike's hatch is open, but he isn't out." Mulholland reports in a hushed voice over the comm, back to the Huron. "Wait a minute. They're slowing down."

"I have Captain Forrester on the line. He's trying to reach the colonel," Campau says. "He wants to speak directly to you, Captain, sir."

"He can't take the message direct to Jackson? We're kind of busy here," Jake replies, more terse than he wants. His head pounds and his chest gripped in a vise. He's sure it is the anxiousness, nervousness of what he intends to do to ruin Pike's day. He watches his rear gunner stop and squat on the hillside.

"I am sorry, sir," Campau hesitates, "He wants to speak with you. Now."

"What are we doing, Captain?" Phelps says as she slows the Huron to a full stop.

Jake can tell by her tone she is sore by the way he speaks to them all.

There is no time for this pettiness.

"Switch me over," he says to Campau.

There is a hiss of static then some garbled voices in the background until Campau patches him direct.

"Captain, you there?" the familiar voice of Frank Forrester comes over the line; the commander of the HTV Ridgerunner Ontario, his voice low, clipped and coarse, like his vocal cords have been rubbed raw by sandpaper. He'd taken a gash across the throat years ago by a local UCRA citizen during a feeding run; sometimes they were a bit anxious to get their dinner.

"Here," Billet replies. "Why isn't my message going up the food chain? I got a serious situation here."

Forrest tries to clear his throat. It doesn't work. "Where're you at? What's your A-O?"

"We're running parallel to Pike in the Maynard pit, bearing southwest."

"Campau informed me a little of what's been going on. I'm having a hard time swallowing it," Forrester says. "Jeremy's right next to Jackson. Hell, I always thought he was bucking for the Colonel's position. It doesn't make sense."

"He fed Felder a line of crap before taking off. Even though they had all the civilians who'd gone in the drink, he kept the big bastard who's carrying what we believe to be Datropoline in his gut and said there was a sixth he had to go get," Jake says as the information swirls in his head. It's hard to keep the thoughts together with the pain and the internal throb. His mind works so fast he has to catch a breath until his heart slows its marathon beat. He wipes moisture from his brow, not rain but cold sweat. Every raised scar on his head and face feel like hot wire. "He popped the civvies he didn't need, and was heading further south when he ran into the group who'd been jamming the airwaves. He fingered Largo and Lettner's loyalists to steer me away and shake the smell of bullshit off him."

"Did he actually say he's bugging out?"

Jake has to think on it, thoughts which flow like molasses. Slow.

"No. No, he didn't admit those were his intentions, but he kept telling me about some classified mission, rubbed it in my face. In fact, the last thing he said was this might be his final mission and not to follow him."

"I'm gonna get my ass chewed for prying, but I'll get with the Colonel and find out if there's something going on, if he or anyone else has set something up with Pike and crew."

"They turned their main gun on us and threatened to nail us if we followed," Billet adds.

"Oh shit," is Forrester's reply. "And you're running beside him?"

"We're running silent. He doesn't know I'm following him."

Jake watches Mulholland rise from his crouch and peer over the embankment, then quickly squats back down.

"You guys are going to hit the Walker-Grandville border," Forrester says. "You need to let him go. We can have Grandville curtail him at the Wilson Outpost until we get this sorted out or can send more armor out there. You need to stand down, Jake."

"Negative."

"What?"

"I'm going to stop him."

Forrester hesitates. "Let me get the Colonel before you do anything crazy."

Jake feels his head spin. The gray clouds overhead aren't doing anything but he feels the storm within churn, racing, gobbling him up.

"Maybe Jackson's in on it too. Maybe he's in bed with Largo, with Pike."

"What in the Hell are you talking about?" Forrester blasts.

Machine gun fire from the roadside breaks Forrester's roar over the receiver.

"I'm spotted." Mulholland, breathless as he rolls down the hillside. He comes up plastered with wet leaves and mud. "Don't know if they made me or think I'm a Feral."

"Billet, gawddamnit, do not…"

Jake switches off his helmet headset. "I'm done talking to Central. Get us over there, Lou."

The Huron roars to life. The front tires try to bite deep into the soggy soil until the rear tracks churn, bite and push the heavy transport forward.

Mulholland takes two steps towards them, and then stops, checks to see if the Devastator is following. The answer comes as twin turbines loudly whine and the nose of the mighty Abrams rises up behind the bank of pines. All track versus the armored transport, it grinds forward slowly, the massive treads rotate and tear into soft earth.

Eddie Mulholland turns to run but his boots get tangled in the underbrush. He throws his hands out, loses the rifle, and goes down hard on his face. Knowing his life depends on it, he pulls himself up, retrieves his weapon.

"Get down!" Jake yells, pumps his open hand, palm down at the gunner.

Mulholland's eyes grow big as saucers as the Huron bears down on him.

The Devastator continues to bite into the hillside.

"Pike's hailing us," Campau shouts from below.

"Fuck him," Billet responds though not loud enough for his navigator to hear.

"I'm slowing to let Eddie jump on," Loutonia says as she steers towards Mulholland.

A few small pine trees suck under the chewing treads of the tank, and it lurches upward; main gun and front end of turret come into view.

"Ram that son of a bitch," Billet shouts, red rage fog his sight, only death on his mind.

Lance Corporal Loutonia Phelps, always a good soldier, though fearful of what is happening now, obeys her commander.

Not wanting to be out in the open, Mulholland runs—a long, lean jackrabbit—back for the hill.

A lone pine snaps and leans forward as the Devastator's front lip mashes it flat.

The Huron roars up the slight incline, catches the top tip of the tree like a lance, bends it over, and snaps it to knife-sized splinters.

With its running start and the 68 ton Devastator nose up on an incline, the 72 ton heavy transport shoves it down. The Huron's huge dual wheels ride up the tank's skirting, and as if the hill creates a launch pad for it, the vehicle comes down atop the Devastator as the tank slides back to the roadbed.

The Huron rolls over the top of the tank. Pike's .50-cal goes sideways, mashes down like a broken nose on the side of the turret's face before coming loose and clatters off the tank to the road below. The wind sensor on the rear of the turret and one of the whip antennae meet their demise. Pike's open hatch, snagged under the body of the transport, bends back on its hinges. The entire tank wheezes and dips under the Huron's weight.

Something pings loudly within and to the side of the Devastator's main gun, and then the transport is over and off, its front wheel axles strain as rubber meets pavement again.

Still going full bore, Loutonia brings the Huron across the road and down the opposite embankment, plowing a small tidal wave of grass, rock and top soil as it goes. Properties long cleared of habitation create a manageable clearing for her. Nimble as driving a sports car but with the destructive elegance of a Mack truck, she goes full throttle into a turn, front wheels spin, right track stops, left track grinds them around to face the direction in which they'd just came. She guns the Huron and starts back up towards Butterworth.

Stokes taps the side of his helmet, motions Jake to switch on his headset.

"The Major demands to talk to you," Campau says through Jake's helmet.

"Open the channel."

"…know what the hell he's doing!" Pike's angry voice blasts loud and clear.

"I'm here, Major," Billet says as the Huron bucks topside and hits the asphalt with a squeal of tires.

"What are you trying to pull, Jacob?" Jeremy snarls over the comm. "I thought I told you not to follow. What kind of goddamned stunt was that?"

Billet can hear klaxons in the background. The Huron must've put a hurting on them with its drive over. He can't help but grin a little, though the action maks his head hurt the more.

"You were coming after my guy, I thought we'd give you a little nudge," Jake answers, "Just to show we aren't backing down. I don't know exactly what's going on here," he continues as Loutonia slows to a stop facing sidelong several yards behind the tank. "But we're going to find out as we're both going to the Wilson Outpost and calling into Central Command."

"Bull. Shit." Pike responds.

The Devastator's turbine engine revs, black smoke pours out in great rolling columns. Jake notices the big Zee wrapped in its beige canvas tarp seize and buck with the rhythm of the tank's engine.

"Orders, Captain?" Loutonia asks, nervous.

Jake opens his mouth to speak. His throat constricts as his chest pinches tight. He grabs at his tactical vest, tries to drive his fingers into his flesh to massage the pain out. Stokes suddenly opens up with the quad .30's, further tensing him.

"The big guy's coming loose!" the gunner exclaims, peppers the side and then rear of the Devastator with machine gun fire. The bullets bounce off the tank's thick hide.

"What're you doing?" Jake can hardly get the words out. He sees the 25mm gun traverse. "No, no, no," he swears.

Bindings thrown free, the Rhino snaps upright, pushes arms and legs out straight, causes the remainder of its cloth prison to unfurl. It immediately goes over and off the back end of the tank, hits the roadway on hands and knees. The landing doesn't bother it as it pushes itself up onto its feet; one foot with boot, the other a dirty, threadbare sock. It stands with chin nearly in line with the top deck of the tank. It sniffs the air with a sneer, revealing jagged teeth and brown-black gums.

More by smell than by sight, the massive Zee turns its head, first peering towards the Huron and then as if looking to the tree line in front of them.

Billet and Stokes look in the direction of the Rhino's gaze.

Mulholland crouches within the low pine boughs, unaware.

The big zomb probably hasn't eaten in days, its usual fare, doped meat which keeps it calm, docile.

The UCRA civilian is near feral state: angry, hungry and eager to kill.

"I told you to stay clear, and you attack me?" Pike bellows over the radio.

The Devastator's 120mm cannon begins to traverse.

Jake grips the hatch ring with one hand, holds his helmet. "Evasive Maneuvers. Go." Before the first word leaves his mouth,

Phelps guns the Huron.

The HTV dives into the opposing off-road hillside; front wheels, then tracks, dig in. The big rig starts up the incline and then hangs there much like the Devastator had. Wheels and tread bite but find no purchase.

Jake watches as the tank's main gun starts to rotate from its full forward position. He can see it firing, blowing them into little pieces, and he and his crew heavenly confetti littering the ground before the Pearly Gates.

The M256 120mm cannon tracks left 30 degrees…

…And stops with an audible squeal and a loud metallic pop. The big barrel wavers back and forth as the turret tries to move in the opposite direction but appears locked in place.

"He's on Mulholland," Stokes yells.

So focused on the tank's activities, Jake thinks his gunner talks about it. When Stokes lays off throwing lead pebbles at the Devastator and trains his guns forward again, that's when the sergeant's words sink in.

Like a grizzly with a lame leg, the Rhino slowly but steadily climbs the hill past the transport, heads towards Mulholland who still focuses on the rumbling Abrams.

The gunner sees the big Zee as it lumbers up within a few yards of his location. He brings his rifle up, fires with pine branches in his face.

The Rhino's left shoulder jerks, but continues unfazed up the hill.

"Get up there!" Stokes bellows as he hesitates to fire the quad's in fear of mowing down his crew mate.

"Watch… the… tank," Billet wheezes. He gulps air until he gets a lungful and holds it as the Huron grinds away beneath him, inching its way forward.

Turret locked 30 degrees to port; the Devastator starts to rotate on its left track, the right churns the weathered and cracked asphalt. The loader's hatch opens a breath, bobs up and down, the person below struggling to push it open. With a final thrust, the iron clamshell goes up and Pike's loader, Corporal A.G. McGraw, pops his head up long enough to survey the top of their turret. There is no smile on his face as he ducks back down and closes the hatch behind him.

Mulholland takes two steps back as the Rhino approaches the crest of the hill. The Zee is well within range for a point blank head shot. Confident this will be over soon, Eddie squeezes the trigger. Nothing happens. He releases and pulls again, swears with the instant realization.

"Guns jammed full of sand," he says more to himself but it comes across the comm.

He slaps at the M4's stock to no avail. He stands up, backs up, turns and starts to run.

The Rhino comes over the lip of the hill far faster than Mulholland is used to seeing from a West Side resident. Eddie pulls his sidearm, fires over his shoulder as he runs across the sandy uneven ground. The bullets hit the big rotter in the chest and neck, misses a head shot that would certainly have put the brute down.

The tip of his boot catches an old log half-buried in the sand, hidden by the tall field grasses. Mulholland flails, miraculously keeps his balance and remains upright, then something else catches his ankle. He goes down on hands and knees. He twists, knowing what has caught him. Kicking with his free foot, the lean gunner plants the hard sole of his boot heel under the Rhino's chin, snapping its head back.

The big Zee lets Eddie loose, its lower jaw flaps loose at its worm-eaten neck. With vocal cords no longer able to utter truly human sound, the Rhino, on its knees, rears back and howls like a wolf under water.

Intent on further distancing himself from the monstrous creature, Mulholland crab crawls as fast as he can before he gets to his feet. He hesitates as the Rhino's tattered orange and black plaid shirt exposes its belly.

The undead giant looks like its abdomen has taken a blow by an I-beam. Probably not the case but there is evidence of somewhat recent surgery, of the man's guts being opened up then stitched back together again. The stitchery runs vertically the entire length of the abdominal cavity, from diaphragm to pelvis, then horizontally below the rib cage and just above the pubic area. The design is well-known amongst the police, military and drug traffickers as it designates the zombie as a carrier of illegal substances for the latter folk.

Within the Rhino's guts, Mulholland surmises, is why the Major is doing what he is doing.

Both living and unliving man turn as the Huron breaks over the hill, carves out a new trail as it flattens everything in its path.

Mulholland sees Stokes at his quad guns and the new 25mm turret gun aimed directly at him. He hopes his crew mate doesn't open fire on them; the Sergeant isn't famous for his accuracy.

A gurgling snarl brings the gunner back to the forefront as the big zomb swipes at him with a tree trunk thick arm. Necrotic flesh flaps like loose strips of dead bark. Eddie sucks in what little gut he has, grimaces as the jagged fingernails slash through tactical vest and underlying fabric. He feels the cold sting of air on the gash left from the strike.

No warm flood of blood, or uncoiled guts, gush from his mid-section, and there is no time to worry about it as the Rhino comes at him with another roundhouse swing.

"Jiminy Christmas, a boxer in your past life?" Mulholland grunts, throws his right arm up, uses the bottom of his pistol's handgrip to take the blow. The impact reverberates through him but saves his forearm from being snapped like a twig. He repays the Rhino in kind by a punch to its skull. He connects solidly and turns the brute's head with an audible pop of cartilage.

The creature disoriented, Mulholland turns and uses his long legs to put distance between them.

The Devastator's main gun discharges, almost stops the gunner in his tracks. A stand of tall pines to the right of the hillside disappear in a rich and roiling burst. A small chunk of woodland is sent to the heavens. Before the shattered earth settles, the big tank punches through the boiling smoke cloud.

Mulholland looks over his shoulder and gasps. Rhino still trails him. He fires again, hits it in the head but only a chunk of ear is blasted away. He swears at himself for his sudden poor aim.

Pock marked by lead shot, the Zee weeps a dirty red jelly of semi-congealed blood. It doesn't have a lower jaw to help it sneer, but crooks its head down and looks under its brow at Mulholland as it closes the gap between them.

"I should've listened to my folks and been a track star," Eddie mumbles as he ejects the spent clip from his pistol.

The Huron grinds along fifty yards behind him with Pike and the Devastator in close pursuit.

Stokes yells over the comm, "Get clear!" as the 25mm gun rotates in slight degrees left and right as he zeroes in on the big zomb.

"The damn thing's going to outrun me just because it doesn't have to breathe." Eddie gasps; his leg muscles aflame. He fumbles with a fresh clip, palms it into his pistol. Soggy from traversing the wet ground and clumped with sand, his combat boots are lead weights tied to his ankles. He can feel an old knee injury start to send small pinpricks of pain radiating from the center of his right leg.

And it gives him an idea.

"Maybe this'll take some steam out of you." He slows, twists at the waist, chest heaving, lungs on fire. He raises his pistol and fires.

The Rhino bawls as its left knee flays backwards. Bits of flesh and bone fall away. It continues forward, staggers, and teeters: a half hewn tree debating if it's going to topple.

Mulholland lifts his pistol, aims higher; the spot between the Zee's eyes in line with his gun sight. He pulls the trigger…

The Rhino disappears in a geyser of flame, smoke and sand.

Mulholland flails backwards, blown back by the explosive upheaval. Chunks of sandy mud, burning grass and wet gray flesh rain upon him in a slanted downpour. A piece of glass slashes across his right hip. He yells in pain. Something tasting like half-cooked hamburger and medicinal foulness enters his open mouth. He lands hard on his back, coughs grit and the rotten, warm gristle. He fumbles at his wounded side, presses his gloved hand against it.

"Damn it! I told you… to stay off that gun," Eddie hears Billet yell through the commlink though the captain's voice sounds strange, weak, far away.

Mulholland turns his head—thankful it's still attached—as the Huron comes around the smoking pile of the Rhino's remains. Stokes seems concerned until he sees him in one piece. The sergeant then broadly smiles and nods his head. The smoking 25mm cannon barrel nods in unison.

"How's that for shooting?" Stokes says as the transport pulls up and stops next to Mulholland. "You owe me, buddy."

Eddie rises slowly, winces as his side throbs. He spits more earth and the earthly remains of the big rotter. His response to his celebratory friend dies as the Abrams, now in the spot the Huron had been when it had fired on the Rhino, shouts its own 120mm cannon response to the scene. The landscape erupts again, many yards behind and beyond the Huron, but the message is clear.

"Can you make it aboard?" Jake leans over the side of the hull, hand outstretched.

"Got hit. Just a scratch I think," Mulholland says as he grabs the rungs, ignores his aching side, and clambers up the side of the Huron, holds tight as Loutonia starts the rig moving again.

Billet clamps a hand onto the gunner's shoulder as he reaches the roofline. "I have ya," he says but groans and lets loose of the man as his chest squeezes the breath from him. Black spots dance before his eyes. He is going to pass out.

"Captain?" Mulholland, concerned, pulls himself the rest of the way up.

"I'm... okay. B-back to your post. We made Pike... a little angry."

Jake eyes the wreckage in the churned up, smoking crater that is the Rhino's final burial place. His face sours. The dead thing's mid-section has been split apart. He's seen his share of gore both of the living and the undead. The wrinkle of disgust doesn't come from the sight of the big body so gnawed away by gun fire a master surgeon wouldn't be able to re-assemble the flesh puzzle.

A glass vial, about the size of a jelly jar, which had been stitched into Rhino's abdominal cavity, lies shattered. Amber liquid pools about the shredded Zee. Billet's seen that saving and cruel substance before: Datropoline, the "vaccine" the government had used on all service men and women when the virus started. It appears someone is anxious to get their hands the substance, the only reason someone would try to smuggle it like a common drug in a Zee. He doubts whoever wants the stuff fully understands its after-effects...or maybe they do.

"Your little trophy, or whatever... you had arranged for it..." Jake hesitates, tries to draw a fresh breath with stubborn lungs. He glances across the tract of land as the Devastator closes the gap. "... looks like it won't be... any good to you now, Major."

Pike roars an atomic blast of expletives across the communications lines. The Devastator turns in a wide arc, moves around the small crater where the smoking, shredded remains of the Rhino lay.

"Superb job you've done," Pike says, a Mount Everest of sarcasm behind the statement. "A year's worth of preparation flushed down the shitter."

The Devastator moves in a clockwise route around the body.

Loutonia maneuvers the Huron in a wider circular course in the opposite direction.

"If we were in any other place," Pike continues, "I'd be pushing for serious misconduct and assault charges for you and your crew, Captain."

Billet opens his mouth to respond. The words won't come. He wants to say the charges could go both ways.

Pike and crew could be issued a BCD—Bad Conduct Discharge—for simply rifling the undead civilians and leaving them afloat out there in the boondocks. Destroying a military outpost, potentially opening the area to intruders, firing upon another crew and vehicle—as they'd just done—smuggling contraband and, to top it off, attempting to go AWOL and steal one of the GRCC's MBT's; grounds for high treason and grave local as well as federal offenses punishable by more extreme means than discharge papers.

'Course, Jake surmises, *disregarding the command of a higher ranking CO, firing upon him, his crew and vehicle, using the Devastator as a big armored stepping stone and badly damaging the vehicle...* Those are grounds to get him a royal ass chewing from Top Brass, and lose the right to command, including the command of the Huron.

The gray clouds break. Tiny slivers of blue sky open and sharp bands of sunlight stab down upon the field, brightening the wet landscape.

More pain lances through Jake's skull, and his body shudders as he turns away, squints, tries to shield his eyes. He doubles over. Stokes notices his struggle and replies to Pike. "And since we aren't anywhere where anyone else can see, you are ready to blow a hole through us?"

Billet draws himself erect again, raises his hand and tries to shut the gunner up. The whine of the Abram's turbine brings his attention back to it. The Devastator starts to turn on tread. With its turret damaged and locked in position, it's the only way to bring their cannon bear on the Huron.

"Tank's main gun… is locked in position." Billet says down into the Huron's cabin as loud as his strained vocal cords will let him. He isn't sure if anyone has recognized the damage to the tank's turret. "Keep us out… of its line of fire."

Stokes spins about, fires his quad .30's at the Abrams. "Ain't going down without a fight," he says as the guns lash out. As the Huron traverses, he sweeps into Mulholland's radius of fire.

Heart still pounding from his recent activities with the Rhino, Mulholland stays off the trigger, doesn't waste the shot. The big armored beehive is already fully disturbed; throwing the equivalent of small lead pebbles at it is a futile action.

Billet grips the hatch coaming, waits for the Devastator to line them up in its sights and fire the killing blow.

Loutonia steers the transport in a slightly tighter arc as Campau directs her towards a series of tall sand berms.

"We make it behind those, and we can fire a TOW at them." Campau says as he peers out the glassed rectangle making up his small front viewport. He leans back, tries to see over Loutonia to keep his eyes on the Devastator.

Loutonia glances at the navigator incredulously. "You don't know much about that tank out there, do you?"

"I'm a MRAP's guy, trained out of Camp Lejeune, in the 126th Cavalry Regiment," Campau replies.

"Courage Sans Peur." Courage without fear, she says in her best French. "Hooah!"

Campau puffs out his chest with pride upon her exclamation.

Loutonia looks over her shoulder out the side port window, watches the Devastator come around. They don't seem to try very hard in getting a bead on her but she isn't going to let them. "If we're pasted by one of their standard rounds, behind a hill of sand or otherwise," she returns her gaze upon Campau, "it'll go through the hill, through us, and maybe detonate in the hill behind, but not before it ignites any ammunition and fuel we carry and sucks us out the exit hole in a fine red mist."

Deflated, Campau utters, "Fuck."

They both wince as the Devastator's machine guns rakes across the Huron's hull.

"I have a crazy idea." Loutonia guns the diesels, tightens her turn as much as she can to draw them out of the line of fire. "Would rather die trying than go up to Saint Peter in a ketchup bottle."

Campau says nothing.

Topside, Billet, Stokes and Mulholland raise their heads cautiously.

"I'll light the fucker up," Stokes warns, turns his head in line with the circling Abram's, the turret with the TOW canister follows his lead.

"Don't. Goddamnit." Jake responds hoarsely. The world turns sideways, grows brighter then darker as if the Almighty plays with the dimmer switch. He blinks, tries to clear his vision. The damnable sunlight sends a lancing pain from his head and down every nerve ending in a tiny rolling ball of needles. His entire body aches horribly.

From below, he hears Loutonia: "Bring us in tight. Don't let them angle in on us. I don't think they'll fire point blank."

"Roger that," Campau replies.

Stokes suddenly howls, "Hey!" and looks down. "What the hell, woman, if you want to get my attention..." His eyes cross and he howls louder—higher pitched—and drops down his hatch hole faster than a spooked gopher.

Loutonia exits the front gunner's hatch with a tail of the sergeant's expletives hanging in the air behind her. Her short, black hair snaps in the wind as the Huron swings around closing the gap between the Devastator. The tank tracks in a tight circle around the transport; its cannon motor hums and gun bounces slightly side to side, trying to break from its locked position. The two vehicles jockey about each other like a pair of wrestlers looking for an angle to pounce and overtake the other. With one of her .45's in hand, she locks her left leg, butts it against the open hatch, and stuffs the toe of her right boot into one of the two roof rungs between the gunner and commander's openings. She withdraws her other .45 and partially squats to maintain her balance.

"What… are you doing?" Jake wheezes; flesh ashen beneath the hot red stripes crisscrossing his face.

Campau brings the Huron in line and a little to the right of the Devastator. The tank turns, moves towards them, the main gun's angle soon to be on target with the big carrier.

"I'm going to end this little family feud between you and Pike," Loutonia says concerned with Jake's ill-appearance, but more concerned with Pike getting a shot off and ending them for good.

The Devastator's coax machine gun opens up, spits lead at the Huron.

Billet ducks as bullets ring off the Huron's side.

Mulholland opens fire from the rear, aims at the tank's viewports with hope the hits keep them from taking out Loutonia.

Stokes pops up as the Abrams and HTV pass side by side. "Crazy bitch," he mutters as Loutonia takes two long strides and goes off the Huron's side.

Loutonia holds her breath as she leaps. A six foot span of empty air lay between the north-facing Huron and the south-pointed Devastator, and an assured breakneck drop to the ground below. She goes across the gap, guns up. She glances down without moving her head, sees the churning tracks and bogies of the tank she'll be ground under if she misses her target. If she lands, loses balance and goes backwards, her own 72 ton rig and its rear tracks will crush her flat.

She also expects Pike or his loader to pop from their turret hatches and shoot her in the face.

Her boots hit the top of the tank turret with a solid *tung*. She throws herself forward to avoid her latter fears of stumbling and falling headlong between the moving vehicles.

With left foot on the gunner's hatch in case he decides to surface, and her right foot pressed against the collar of Pike's open and mangled hatchway, Loutonia draws her .45's together. She takes a breath and jams the barrels into the dark turret rabbit hole. For a second she thinks about spouting some clichéd bad action movie one-liner, but as the Devastator rolls forward, starts to spin and turn its cannon on Huron's departing backside, the brief humor of it leaves her.

"Stop the damn tank."

She sees the top of Pike's helmet in the dull green glare of the internal turret control electronics. He cocks his head upwards as she flips the safety off both guns.

"Or what, *Corporal* Phelps?" Pike sneers, points at the golden oak leaf insignia on his helmet.

It gave her all the resolve in the world.

"Or I'll unload both guns in the Devastator's bowels. A swarm of lead bees the sting I doubt you'd enjoy."

Pike hesitates, and then says, "Full stop," in which the Devastator abruptly halts.

Loutonia quickly adjusts her footing as she's nearly dislodged.

"Larsen. You asshole," she says loud enough for the tank driver to hear.

"You realize what kind of trouble you're getting yourself in, acting upon the whims of your commander? Captain Billet, that is." Pike clarifies.

He starts to rise, raising his hands the best he can within the confines of the turret housing. She slides the .45's further into the hole, further at him.

He sits back down.

"Jake didn't tell me to do any of this," she replies. She drops the formalities. They are all friends here, well, parting acquaintances unless she can detour the Major.

In the background, Loutonia hears the rumble of the Huron's diesel turbines rev and the sound of the vehicle coming back her way.

"I am sure it wasn't you who decided to follow us when I ordered you to turn back," Pike slowly rises again, hands still raised. "I'm sure you weren't the one who ordered the ambush and drive your rig over us, try to shut us down."

Loutonia doesn't answer. Pike knows. She aims her pistols, ready and steady, leveled in Pike's face.

"You guys did quite some damage to the Devastator," he says, rising so his upper body shows, hands remain up.

"Sorry about that. Hope wherever you're heading off to can fix things up," she says taking a step towards the rear of the tank turret, out of the line of fire if Pike's gunner—Mitch Davison—decides to make a trick shot up through open turret hatch.

The Huron rolls closer. Pike's eyes follow it but Loutonia's stay on him.

"You're intent on leaving?" she asks him. Considering her annoyance with him, she doesn't like the thought of losing another vehicle, especially a big gun rig like the Devastator. There are rumors of more arms, men and vehicles coming up once the old rail lines from Kalamazoo and New Holland to Grand Rapids are secure, but there are never any real promises of anything in this day and age. Men and machine, like Pike and crew, turn their backs on their city and fellow soldiers for other fame and fortune nowadays.

"I'm intent on leaving," Pike replies. "We *are* on a mission. I've tried to explain this to your hard-headed captain, but he insists on being the hero and getting his balls in a boil." Pike returns his gaze upon her, and the weapons pointed in his face.

She eases off the triggers a hair. "I don't know all you two's history, but if this whole thing is what this is about—" Maybe she needs to shoot both Jake and the equally bull-headed TC. "The Lettner mission didn't turn out a win-win for everybody as you well know. And it's something Jake deeply regrets in certain ways, it brought him through some inner hells I think he addressed and moved on from, and it still affects him today."

Pike inserts: "It's not all that," not all full of his usual bluster to Loutonia's surprise. However, he quickly changes face and glares at her with open contempt. "But I gave an order. You didn't follow. Now we're here. What are your intentions, Corporal?"

She thinks on this. Initial intentions were to talk Pike into aborting whatever outside plans he has and return to Grand Rapids. Her thoughts on bringing man and machine under house arrest for trying to defect and steal from the GRCC, well, with the out-gunned Huron against the Abrams killing machine: it is futile and promises an assured ticket to the pearly gates.

"I'm just trying to keep you from blowing a hole in us," Loutonia says.

"Ought to," Pike snorts. "You seriously put a gaping hole in our plans." He pats the skin of the turret before him and nods towards the blasted remains of the Rhino. The glass shards from its broken belly jar sparkle in the spreading sunlight. He again looks at the Huron which pulls up parallel to the tank.

"I'll let this one transgression pass as I really hold nothing against *you*, Corporal," Pike says. "But you should tend to your Captain. He doesn't appear to be doing well."

Pistols still trained on Pike, Loutonia glances over her shoulder. "Oh God." Her arms drop, fingers off the triggers, .45's go holstered in an eye blink.

She leaps from the tank, boots bite into the soft sand as she lands. With four long strides she makes it across the short gap between vehicles, and throws herself onto the rungs going up the Huron's left side. As her hand meets the roof line's top rung, it touches Jake's lolled head as he lies halfway in and halfway out of his commander's hatch.

"What happened?" Loutonia cries, panic in her voice as she shoulders Billet's head and works on bringing him gently upright.

Mulholland is already there, kneeling on the steel plate behind the hatchway though he appears hesitant to touch their downed commander.

"Help me," she snaps at the gunner as he reaches to assist.

Stokes stands rigid at his station, quad guns pointed at Pike and the Devastator. He activates the 25mm gun turret. It grinds on its bearing ring, cannon quivering slightly left and right, up and down, as it follows his head movement.

"Don't know. He was watching you then suddenly went staring off into the distance," Stokes explains without eyes leaving their opponent. Pike stands in clear view, watches. The gunner can't tell if the serious look on the TC's face is one of concern or bored indifference. "He started babbling and then keeled over like a sack of potatoes."

Loutonia brings one leg up onto the roof line, balances with one stiff, strong leg and foot on the steel rung. She loops Jake's right arm over her left shoulder, his head rests against her chest. "Captain. Jake, talk to me." She can feel the heat his fevered flesh emits and, with some relief, can feel the beat of his heart; a small hammer against her body.

"Jenna, don't come here," Jake says in a tiny breathless voice. "Keep Joey away. Don't... come here." He lifts his head, looks over Loutonia's shoulder, his gaze upon some distant point out along the rolling slopes of the gravel pit.

Loutonia turns his head so he will look directly at her. Their eyes meet. His pupils are dilated, way too large. The many battle scars crisscrossing his pale face appear like red worms; the deep stripe across his forehead he received last September stands out: a discolored bruise versus an old healed wound.

"Jake, do you know where you are?" she asks.

His eyes seem to focus on her; a feeble smile split his pale complexion. "In a gravel pit southwest of town. Wet, cold." He takes a raspy breath. "I think... I think I'm dying, Jenna."

Her heart sinks.

His hand reaches up and takes a fist of her shirt sleeve. "Lou, you gotta get me out of here," Jake says in a small voice. He holds her like it is the only thing anchoring him to this plane of existence. His heart beats; a thunder clap in ears and chest. He feels conflicting waves of heat and cold wash over his body, no longer able to discern if it is the rainy drizzle from the damnable sky, heat from Loutonia, the Huron, or his body totally fubar'd. He suspects the latter. In his head, thoughts of giving up, breaking down, of fighting to hang on, battling through, of killing everyone and rending the flesh from their bones, giving himself up to be torn asunder by the crazy world: yes, fucked up beyond all recognition.

Loutonia feels him further sag against her.

"Is he going to be okay?" Pike says in everyone's commlink.

The Devastator revs, twin exhausts ruffle the wet sand and bend the field grass.

"Don't know. He seems in a bad way," Loutonia answers, looks over her shoulder at the tank. Pike starts to duck back below, eyes still on them.

"Get him back to the BTF, or back to the city." Pike's head disappears below the turret deck.

"And what're you doing?" she says as the big Abrams starts to turn on tread, away from them, to the southwest, towards the road which will take them further away from the city.

"Leaving," Pike replies, "to our next destination, though I am sure—" The Devastator lunges forward, spits a small rooster tail of sand, chewed gravel and grass, and begins to track quickly away. "—I'm sure we'll meet again." Tone not all friendly, yet not totally sinister.

Stokes snarls, "Why that son of a…"

"Don't you fire at them," Loutonia warns Stokes. She looks at Mulholland who kneels beside Billet. "Help me get him down below," she says to him. "Campau, I need you topside."

"Aye, ma'am," Campau says from below.

"I'm second-in-command if the captain is down," Stokes peers at Billet whose eyelids flit and mouth mumbles something so faint not even Loutonia or Mulholland can make heads or tails of it. Inwardly, the gunner has never seen Billet in such a way, on his last leg, and though he means to talk tough, his guts churn like a blender on puree.

Loutonia glares at Stokes, and then fully looks to Mulholland. "Get his helmet off," she says glancing down at Jake's helmet with the black words BILLET stenciled across the front. "Corporal, we're coming down," she says to Campau.

***

Lying in the tall wet grass on a ragged tree-lined bluff overlooking the gravel pit, runny eye to scope, Black Hair watches the Abrams peel away and the dark-skinned HTV driver run back to the transport. The words repeating in his head keep him on task; keep his gray-fleshed finger on the trigger of his rifle but not firing. The meatless rear gunner keeps getting in his way, and then the woman as they coddle his ragdoll target.

"What's wrong with you, Billet?" Tortured vocal cords emit, sounding normal inside his head, but emitted in a wet gurgle as if spoken underwater.

He can see the transport's crew-meat start to take their captain below into the vehicle's hold. They remove his helmet. No matter. The shot can be made with or without such protection. The captain's bristly scalp is revealed though: soft outer flesh, bullet-breakable bone case and soft gray matter brain-meat center.

The scope reticle aligns.

Trigger eases back.

Billet disappears into the carrier's hold.

***

"Drop that bench and lay him down," Phelps says to Mulholland as they carry Billet down into the Huron's belly. Mulholland holds him with arms looped under Jake's bent knees. Jake's helmet lays in the crotch of his bent legs against the gunner's chest, while Loutonia holds him with her arms slung under Jake's armpits.

Eddie uses the tip of his right foot to grab at the stanchion bar of one of the longer dropdown benches. He unlatches it. Able to handle four people tightly packed, the long, thin-cushioned seat drops into an open position with a metallic clang.

"Is there anything I can do?" Campau asks as the other two lay Billet on the bench and begin securing him. Billet's helmet falls to the metal floor grate with a dull thud.

Jake wheezes and lifts a hand towards the young navigator, makes raking motions. "No test facility," he rasps at Campau though his eyes roll up into the back of his head as he speaks.

Loutonia crouches at Jake's side. She takes his hand. It feels deathly cold. "I know, I know. Never there. No worries, Captain," she says. "We're taking you home."

Jake seizes, pinches Mulholland's fingers between his chest and the strap secured across his chest. The gunner jumps back, stumbles over his own feet.

"We have Ferals coming in from the northeast. They must've heard the commotion of the guns," Stokes says over the radio.

"Get up there and man the 30," Loutonia directs Campau. "You and Stokes are on Overwatch. Eddie will see to the captain," Mulholland blanches at this as he steps back towards Billet. "I'm bringing us back to the city."

"Yessir," Campau salutes, starts to turn to the commander's hatch. He stops and turns back. "I don't have a helmet. Idiot up there made me lose mine when we were fetching those civilians from the drink," he says, referring to Stokes.

The bark of quad caliber-.30's sounds from above.

"We better get moving!" Stokes yells over the tumult of guns.

Loutonia scoops up Jake's helmet and hands it to Campau. "Get up there," she says as Campau snatches the helmet up and starts to don it, turns back to the commander's cupola. She looks at Mulholland who crouches next to Billet. He digs through one of the medical pouches. "I think I have one medi-stim injection left."

"Hold… them. I don't need…" Jake's head lolls sideways. He passes out.

Mulholland lifts his hand from the bag, comes up with two sterile, plastic-wrapped epi-pens.

"Give him one now," Loutonia points. "I don't know what's ails him, but give him one now. Then another maybe when we get back into the city enclosure."

Mulholland nods.

Campau tightens down his lid and rises up into the commander's hatch. He grabs the grips of the Cailber-.30, swings it around in the direction Stokes already fires; a half dozen FZ's scramble their way with the gravel pit and ragged tree-lined bluff beyond them.

The Huron's diesels cough to life.

"Hell, yeah!" Campau fingers start to depress the triggers on the machine gun. "This is what I'm talking about!"

Stokes turns his head to frown at the excited navigator.

The captain has risen again, Black Hair thinks within his rotted skull.

The helmet is back on, and, wiping bloody pus from his

scope eye, he can read the black stenciled letters on the front of the headgear: BILLET.

He cannot waste the opportunity, or the shot he's been waiting so long to take.

Eye to scope. Sight on the first "L" on the captain's helmet.

"For you, Mr. Largo," Black Hair hisses, and pulls the trigger.

Stokes turns his head to frown at the excited navigator.

The Huron lurches forward.

Krak-kow! A report from a big rifle sounds in the distance.

Campau snaps backwards, twists violently to the right as if slapped by the hand of God. Like a piece of rubber hose bent back and then released, he comes forward again, nearly clocks himself on the grips of the .30. His brain registers a splash of warm wet rain on the side of his face. He can't get his right hand to come up and wipe the heavy drizzle away, so he uses his left. Taking his left hand off the machine gun, he runs his fingers over his face and then looks at his dripping hand.

It is red with blood.

"He's hit! Fuck, Campau's hit!" Stokes yells, firing his quad guns with one hand while he tries to reach across to Campau.

"I'm fine," Campau says, glances down at his right hand which he can't make move.

His right sleeve is empty, shredded to nothing just below the shoulder, revealing only a portion of his bicep that drips: a downturned can of chili. His eyes follow the blood trail which meanders off behind him.

"Son of a bitch! Son of a bitch!" Stokes screams, his voice grows farther and farther away as the steady pum-pum-pum of the 25mm cannon fires into the hillside.

Campau's face drains of blood as he finds his right arm lays several feet away on the top of the Huron's cargo bay doors. The arm's severed end oozes; impact-torn muscle, vein and flesh in a mangled pile like it's been shoved in a meat grinder.

Stokes still yells, reaches for him.

Campau's blood gushes red. His world goes black.

Chapter Eight
Undead End

"We're a quarter way into the 105 days of summer," the radio announcer says, cheery in her air-conditioned studio. "Grand Rapids is going to see another very hot July week of temperatures in the upper 90's, possibly 100 by week's end." Her tone wouldn't be so cheery if she were down on the street in the middle of the concrete jungle.

"From the torrential rainfall we had this Spring, now this heat, I can say summer has fireballed into West Michigan for sure," the other DJ exclaims, his tone also sugar coated. "The inner city and her west side inhabitants will remain toasty. Just be sure to break out the air-fresheners when the winds come from the west later on today."

"I live in the Plaza Tower, yeah, the scent gets a little ripe off the UCRA. Such is life." The female DJ adds.

"Or... unlife," her companion jabs with a chuckle.

"Right," she replies, cheeriness gone. "It's 10 pm. Now we have some vintage Van Halen, from 1981, *Mean Street* on 105.9 WPJW."

Loutonia turns off the radio. "Living it. Don't need to keep being reminded of it," she says to the silent radio.

She looks out the hospital room window, the A/C unit blows cool air her perspiration-moist body, makes her shiver.

Downtown Grand Rapids, where most of the 90,000 living populace reside, from the tall barricaded riverfront and up the eastern hill to the outposts along College, do all they can to keep cool both physically and emotionally. A few homes on the hill, abandoned for years, have been torn down; concrete-lined basements turned into makeshift swimming pools. Any spot of grass lay brown and crunchy underfoot. The city's electrical system teeters on blowing a major fuse with all the A/C units and emergency-installed air filtration system taxing it. Within the last few weeks as the system did overload, Mayor Honeywell declared controlled "brown-outs" within each city ward to keep it from a total burn out.

People protest the brown-outs. The mayor warns without sustained power, the inner gates that keep the West Side unliving folk from strolling the city streets cannot be kept secure, and the outer perimeter gates—the electrified ones—won't keep outsiders, living or otherwise, deterred.

Still people complain and grow fiery, anger-wise, under the summer broil. Small groups take to protesting, complaining about what the mayor is and isn't doing for the city currently, including any foibles Honeywell may have succumbed to in the past— the biggest one being "his decision" to bring the late NSC High Commissioner, William Lettner, to justice without their consent.

Teeth gnash, angry growls and blood-letting ensue, and this all on the living, civilized city streets while the UCRA populace mills about along the fence line, content in their doped state. The Zees act oblivious to the heat though the military is often called out to hose them down, try to lessen the rotting meat stink and, on occasion, clean up a civilian who's succumb and lay in a maggot-ridden stew of its own juices.

"I don't think declaring martial law and a 9 PM curfew, especially on gorgeous summer evenings, does much good for us

Grand Rapidians," Doctor Frederick Paulson says entering the air-conditioned ICU room pulling Loutonia from her focus out the room's single window.

Loutonia turns toward the doctor and winces against the sharp triple report of someone firing a rifle down amidst the city streets. The sound echoes through the tall buildings all the way up Spectrum Mile where the main and largest hospital in West Michigan stands like a giant square peg buried in the hilltop. She peers out the window again, westward towards downtown central. She sees the red and blue flash of lights from the GRPD Humvees. Searchlights lance into the night sky and rake across buildings.

She turns back towards the doctor with little expression, "We get what we ask for. If we're going to act like animals, then we're going to be treated like animals."

Paulson wrinkles his nose at the statement. From under his arm he pulls a slim electronic tablet, opens it. He swipes his finger along the touch screen, and replies, speaking softly as if under his breath, though not soft enough: "Easy for you to say in your air-conditioned barracks and vehicles."

Taking a step from the window towards the bed before her, her leg bumps against the single chair on that side of the room, ruffles a copy of the Grand Rapids Herald; the front page headline: REGANSHIRE SPLITS FROM GRAND RAPIDS INFLUENCE WHILE BOASTING NEW INDUSTRY AND ARMED FORCES.

Lower on the page, a smaller news item read: RAIL LINES OPEN BETWEEN G.R. AND MUSKEGON. COMMISSIONER HOLTROP OFFERS ASSISTANCE TO BELEAGURED HONEYWELL.

Hands on the butts of her .45's, Loutonia snarls, "I think your sources of information on *that* are way wrong. You ever sit all day in a 72 ton metal box in this heat? The air blows hot because *it's* pissed *it* can't get cool."

Still flipping through his tablet, the blue screen reflects in his glasses multi-colored graphs and scrolling lists of black text, he replies: "I'm sorry. It's been a rough day. The Third Ward got its brown-out date switched to Tuesdays. Wife's seven months pregnant. I didn't get much sleep last night."

Her earpiece squelches. She presses a finger to it, turns it down.

Deciding not to rip the man's head off, her voice softens: "Been there, done that." *A million years and another life time ago it seems.* It brings the aching memory of her children, death, and the man lying in the hospital bed before her.

She steps closer to the bed, looks at all the tubes, the wires, running from bottles and bags and monitors. She looks at the barely breathing form tucked under the starch white sheets. She picks up the left hand lying across the faint rising chest, careful not to tug on the IV line inserted into the ashen flesh; flesh that feels as chill as the sterile room.

"Can I have a few minutes alone with him?" she asks; tone softer.

Paulson glances at his tablet, then at his watch. He taps a button on the tablet, then he tucks it under the arm of his lab coat. "Sure. We'll need to talk though." He looks down at the body in the bed between them. "It's time some decisions were made."

Loutonia grits her teeth, feels the anger rise. She knows it is out of hopeless frustration, not aimed necessarily at the doctor.

Shoulders slump. "Yes. I know. Just give me a few, please."

Paulson nods, does a quick check of the monitors, and leaves the room.

Setting the newspaper on the floor, Loutonia pulls the chair up close to the bed and sits. Not letting go of the hand in her hers, she leans over and presses her lips to the cool, pale flesh. She looks into the face of her captain, her friend, her lover.

"I'm sorry, hon. I've been away for a bit," she says, gently strokes Jake's hand, "Been crazy busy times since we got back."

More gun fire in the depths of the city, muffled like a string of firecrackers going off in the distance.

"We rounded up about half the ZT's from the test facility after their break. You probably don't remember but we had a helluva time getting back. Between the rain and the flooding, guess they got agitated between Pike and us coming through. Damn near destroyed the whole north entrance and enclosure."

Jake does not respond. A breathing apparatus masks half his face, hooked up to what looks like a machine with a small billow in the center. It gently pumps up and down, working his lungs which will not work themselves. A thick line runs down and under the collar of his hospital gown to sensors on his chest, monitors his weak heartbeat.

"Colonel Jackson still gets ridden hard for losing Pike and the tank. Largo is doing most of the bitching and Honeywell's just trying to maintain. I think he's ready to throttle the Treasurer."

She takes a breath, holds it, and lets it out before she continues.

"Supposedly there's more armor coming down from Grayling, but we haven't heard for certain. The city is so far up the GRCC's ass the Colonel can't move on anything without meeting with Honeywell, Largo and the rest of the commissioners."

She isn't sure if somewhere in there Jake is listening. It is somewhat of a comfort to simply talk to him regardless.

She places her left hand over her right, fully clasps his limp hand. The dialysis machine re-circulating his blood hums as it activates; she feels the vibration through their handhold. She watches as fresh, bright red blood flows through the small inlet tube, and the red-black blood—the dying sludge inside him—as it courses back out.

"Mulholland says hello. He's helping to retrofit and up-armor the Huron and Ontario, well, when he's not out hunting the sniper, or snipers, who shot Campau and several others. The person is still at large." She shakes her head in exasperation. "The Colonel pushed for the upgrades on several vehicles. The mayor approved, but Largo's making sure the GRCC gets the flak saying we're squandering the city's capital."

Police car sirens wail in the distance.

"Speaking of Colter, has he been by to see you? He blasted through Rehab and PT. Says his prosthetic is almost better than the real thing." She forces a laugh, more for Jake's benefit than hers.

Jake doesn't respond.

It has been three months but she can still hear the shot, still see Campau, his arm hanging by a bloody strap of skin and muscle. If the Huron hadn't moved when it did Campau would've lost his head versus an arm. The shooter hadn't been caught though Stokes had set the tree-lined bluff ablaze with 25mm cannon fire. The uproar back in the city regarding the incident lived on as someone continued the sniping activities: three GRCC outpost guards, two soldiers and five UCRA civvies during a feeding run. Four inner city civilians counted as casualties of the elusive shooter.

Jake's heart monitor pings dully. The dialysis machine whirs. The single billow of the oxygen machine huffs slowly, its accordion-shaped diaphragm collapses then rises, then collapses, then rises. Loutonia holds his hand, grips it tightly, wills some of her life force through that grip, into him so he comes to, comes back.

She knows it doesn't work that way.

Paulson has been Billet's attending physician since they'd brought him in. After a battery of tests, the doctor concluded the vaccine the captain received, like everyone in the armed service when the Blight arrived, had simply run its course.

From what Loutonia understood, with the Datropoline vaccination and the physiology of some soldiers, they can experience a career of resistance to wounds received by the undead populace. Others, if not fortunate to be totally mutilated in combat, can become sick and Turn. It was the one major reason Datropoline was discontinued and banned by the military. A late four-star general had a bright idea and amended the enlistment contract, using the turned service men and women as undead infantry.

On active duty before the H7N9 outbreak, Billet had been a M113 and M1130 Stryker Command Vehicle driver. He stepped up into a CO position when the Ridgerunner-class HTV's were rolled out. He'd been in dozens of close-quarter scraps with the undead. He mentioned often to Loutonia his surprise at not succumbing as he watched several of his military cohorts fall.

She looked at her own arms; her dark brown skin striped pink with old scars.

"I hope, if this is it for us, I follow you soon." She leans over and presses her warm full lips against the algid flesh of his forehead.

The door to the room opens as she kisses him.

"Goddamnit, doc, I said give me…"

She sucks in her words and snaps upright out of her chair. The chair skids backwards across the linoleum floor and bangs against the sill of the window behind her.

"Sir!" she says, left hand at her side, her right strikes her forehead in a salute.

Frank Forrester, captain of the HTV Ontario, stops within the doorway surprised at Loutonia Phelps sudden exclamation. He clears his throat as he slips the beret off the gray stubble of his balding head. His complexion a shade darker than hers, he stands in full military regalia: olive drab beret and shirt, cammo pants and black boots; except these aren't his field clothes.

Loutonia can tell he's come from a meeting.

"At ease, Corporal." Forrester waves a hand at her to relax. The radio on his belt chirps. He turns the audio down. "Considering where I came from, you aren't standing before a tribunal."

She relaxes, pulls the chair back bedside. She doesn't sit down but takes up Jake's hand again. "What now?' she asks the captain of one of the two remaining Ridgerunner-class HTV's in the city's arsenal.

Forrester walks with heavy strides to the bed, looks down at Billet. His shoulders droop lower as if they've taken a heavier burden than what already weighs upon them.

"Honeywell and Largo, holey fire fight, never been in such a heated meeting," Forrester says over the medical equipment pings, chirps and whirs. "Largo went and put a call into some political friends in Chicago, took cash out of city's coffers to pay for additional troop support without Honeywell or the council's permission. I thought he and Honeywell were going to come to blows. I definitely see now Largo is bucking for the mayor position."

Loutonia thinks Largo is an ass, plain and simple, though she hasn't thought much on his ambitions. She heard what Pike had said three months ago while they were out of earshot from the city. She thought at the time the TC was just on a rant, talking shit as he was on his way out of the place and didn't give a rat's ass.

Maybe there was something to it, something Pike knew that they didn't.

As Loutonia opens her mouth to comment, Forrester says the words first. "Not sure why he'd want the headache."

She closes her mouth and nods.

"Reganshire wants to go head-to-head with us." Forrester continues, "From the Intel we've gathered we have Lettner loyalists both within *and* outside the city." He absently scratches an old scar which runs across the right side of his head. "And the folks in the city don't like the brown-outs, though I think everyone knows *why* it has to be done."

"They're scared of the dark. They think the gates will be compromised when the power is out," Loutonia finishes for him.

She knows. She's heard the complaints over the last month and a half since the mayor and the city council ordered the activities. She can't count the times she's had to explain to paranoid citizens the GRCC maintained three times the security on all major entry points during brown-outs.

But the hard feelings against the GRCC aren't nearly as bad as they are regarding how people perceive the mayor and how he is handling things. Not that she thinks he is doing a bad job. He has always done what has to be done, made the hard choices as he is the top man.

There seems to be a poison coursing through the internal workings of the city. Even with the Blight, the city remained strong, but now something chews and picks at it. The more Loutonia thinks on the events leading up to recent times, starting with the apprehension of the late NSC Commissioner, she can't help but wonder if Largo or someone else stirs the pot, is up to no good, and is creating this unneeded turmoil and dissension in the ranks of city *and* military members.

"So, now, since the west shore rail line is back in service, the city is paying for some Muskegon troops and armament to come in. And now Largo's troops from Illinois…" Forrester sighs, wearily shakes his head.

Billet's heart monitor alarm suddenly beeps loud and rapidly.

Forrester steps back from the bed as if he's the cause.

Having been through it before, Loutonia tightens her grip on Jake's hand.

"Excuse me," Doctor Paulson enters the room with his tablet underarm, almost runs into Forrester. He steps to the monitor, checks the read-outs and presses a red button on the bottom of the heart monitor, killing the alarm. He looks at Loutonia, and then turns to Captain Forrester. "His arrhythmia causes havoc with the machine." He puts his hand out. "I am sorry, Captain. I didn't see you come in."

The two men shake. Paulson pulls his tablet out, taps up an entire screen full of charts and graphs.

Loutonia leans forward, tries to see what is on the screen. She is only able to read the top line which consists of Jake's full name and patient identification number.

"How's he doing?" Forrester asks looking down at Jake.

The respirator huffs but the downed transport commander's chest doesn't appear to rise.

"No change." Paulson scans the tablet screen though he doesn't review any one thing for very long. He sighs. "Listen, Captain, I know you, and especially the corporal, don't want to hear this, but we're closing on the three month mark. Captain Billet isn't going to come around, not in any semblance of his normal self anyway."

Forrester shoots a glance at Loutonia who glares at the doctor. She loses some steam as the CO's forlorn look tells her there are some things that can't be changed.

"I know the City Council and the GRCC are still determining if the Butterworth Test Facility is still viable after the troops rioted," the doctor says, folds the tablet closed and tucks it back under his arm. "I have a temporary *outside* facility we can work on him. This will be a good opportunity for us as Captain Billet will be the first commander who hasn't been fully consumed and had to be put down."

Loutonia snaps. She flies around the bed and takes Paulson by the collar of his scrubs before either he or Forrester can react. She stands an inch taller than the doctor but pulls him up eye to eye, so close their nose tips almost touch.

"That's all he or any other soldier is to you? A piece of meat to experiment on and throw to the wolves?" she snarls, twists a handful of his shirt in her balled fist. "I know it's not common knowledge that you were part of the BTF start-up team. If more people knew I'm sure your patient list wouldn't look so pretty."

Paulson looks at Forrester.

"Corporal. Lou…" The transport captain steps towards her.

"You know what the doctor is suggesting is *not* what Jake wants," Loutonia says, starts to lessen her grip on Paulson. "You know he wouldn't want to go out this way no matter what state or condition he's in."

Forrester stops his advance, looks again at Billet. They are soldiers. They are friends. They all made a pact outside of earshot of their superiors. They have seen what their fallen brethren endure though those men and women are beyond pain and life.

"He signed the enlistment contract amendment as did you," Paulson says to Loutonia, "and you." To Forrester. "If you can provide me with something else that says otherwise..."

Frank Forrester looks down, sees Loutonia's free hand drop to one of her sidearms, flipping the strap on the holster. He sees the corporal glance at Jake as the heart monitor pings hesitantly, the respirator huffs with a slow drawn-out breath and the dialysis machine whirs with its tubes of bright red blood and oily black. She chews her lip, desperately in debate over her next actions. Forrester's hand slips to his own sidearm; not sure if she's going to turn the gun on Jake, him or the doctor.

"Don't do this," Forrester says as tears fill her eyes and roll down her cheeks. "Don't do this. Not here. Not now."

She eases off her grip.

Paulson gulps breath like he's been held underwater and finally let up for air. He rubs at his collar, brows furrowed, anger in his eyes. He steps away from her.

"Time is of the essence. If we wait until his entire system shuts down..." Paulson starts.

"Goddamnit, I'm not listening to this right now," Loutonia yells, balls her fists and clasps them to the sides of her head.

She roughly elbows by the doctor and stomps from the room. Chairs clatter in the hallway and the gasp of a surprised orderly is heard as Loutonia storms down the hall.

"Don't do anything yet without her approval. The captain and her are together, if you know what I mean," Forrester says to Paulson.

"Yes, it is obvious, but I have my orders also. You understand what has to be done. I'd treat you with the respect you deserve if it came to yourself in a similar situation as him," Paulson says, eyes on Billet. "You guys are our only hope, living or not, and your armed populace isn't growing much if you haven't noticed. The effect of the vaccine was a mistake, yet somewhat a blessing in disguise. It keeps the defenders defending to the very end, and we need you more than ever these days in whatever form we can take you."

A semi-living automaton to keep the monsters both living and unliving from your throats, Forrester thinks, yeah, I get you.

A muffled explosion rattles the entire room. The lights shake, flicker, and go out. The men are cast in total darkness. Shouts and shrieks of fear and confusion sound outside in the hallway. A dull emergency light illuminates the corridor outside the room.

"What the hell?" Forrester exclaims as the pop-pop-pop of semi-automatic gun fire is heard outside the building and in the distance.

Paulson hurries from the room, yells orders to the other medical personnel.

Billet's life support apparatus beeps in alarm. The respirator stops in half pump. The dialysis machine goes silent.

Captain Frank Forrester looks beyond the bed, outside into the night time gloom of the summer-boiled city. To the southwest edge of town, just beyond the Eastbank Towers, he sees the red flash of fire illuminating the buildings.

"This can't be good." He grabs his radio from his waist belt. He looks down one last time at Jake. "We'll be back to settle things the right way, buddy. Don't you worry."

The quake of the explosion turned the heart monitor around, it faces the opposite direction.

The HTV Ontario's CO doesn't notice the silent Huron CO's monitor reveals a long flat line.

"This is Forrester. I need a Sitrep of the burst near the Fulton Outpost," the captain says as he hurries from the room and into the hallway of panicked hospital personnel.

***

Thunder in the distance.

Eyes snap open. Only darkness.

Something in throat, nostrils, choking.

Jake sits upright, disoriented, grabs at soft fabric near his hands.

What is this? A cot? A bed?

He yanks out what is in his throat and nostrils. Plastic tubing?

"Hello?" he calls. The words come out low, raw. He clears his throat, and says again, "Hello? Lou? James? Anybody?"

His ears pick up the sound of frantic voices. "Check each patient," someone yells. "We've no power in the west wing," someone else shouts. Running footfalls, overly loud to his freshly awakened senses, he has the urge to scream for silence.

Dry hinges squeal. The thick wood door emits a soft clap as it closes. The ruckus from outside the room diminishes to a bearable nuisance.

"I'm in a hospital?" Jake clears his throat again; vocal cords taut and sandy.

A mingle of strong odors wrinkle his nose. An antiseptic smell threatens to tornado his head around. Medicinal, chemical smells. Sweat, blood and meat aroma: fresh and fetid.

Gun fire turns his head to where his recovering eyesight brings the image of a pulsing window-sized red square. He squints, blinks, and tries to get a clearer view of what he looks upon.

More weapons fire—muffled behind glass, steel and mortar—pull spectral images from his mind and places them on the gossamer canvas before him: planes drop out of a rainy sky; the UCRA surge over the riverbank enclosure, a tsunami of flesh; the brutish undead Rhino throws soldiers about like straw in the wind—Mulholland in the midst of them; nuns and Reganshire slavers playing tug-o-war with an unfortunate West Side shambler; faces of zombitized GRCC men and women clawing and howling at him; Jeremy Pike raging and then laughing atop his big tank turret pulpit. A short yet extensive mental movie outlined in a crimson-hued haze.

Frustrated with the dreary eyesight, he lifts his hands to his face, feels further cords and tubes fall away from his arms. He rubs at his eyes, the action makes them burn. He drops his hands and finds clarity improved.

A titter of female laughter draws his attention to the foot of his bed, to the nearby corner of the room, lit only by the dull red pulse which comes from the sheer curtains of the room's single window. His eyes take a moment to adjust to the darkness there. Further dry hinges squeal as the skinny door of a tall storage closet opens, reveals the outline of Jake's Class "A" uniform within.

But it isn't the uniform, used for formal ceremonies and funerals, which draws his focus, makes his mind scream with madness and despair.

"Hello, Jacob," William Lettner smiles broadly, sitting in the hospital chair in the corner. He acts right at home.

The dead NSC Commissioner sits dressed in a black suit and white shirt like he's just attended a political ball. His collar is unbuttoned and hangs loose, reveals a thick red rope burn around his throat.

The tittering female laughter comes from Rebecca Regan who sits on Lettner's left knee. Her milk-white tresses wave like silk thread in a phantom breeze, curls serpentine about her pale oval face as she peers at him with black, empty sockets for eyes. A hodge-podge of dirty white linen clings to her skeletal frame, the tattered gown reveals more skin than Billet wants to see. The upper portion of her outfit shows shriveled breasts and gangly arms festering with weeping sores. Her lower portion exposes the near-translucent flesh of her thighs and long, spindly legs as she scissors them open and closed. She cackles and weeps—those terrible puckered lids—with insane glee.

Jake looks away and across at the other woman seated upon Lettner's right knee.

"Jenna," Billet moans.

His dead wife sits without emotion opposite the crazed Reganshire woman. She teeters slightly back and forth, her ragdoll arms rest limply in her lap. The toes of her bare feet press against the floor and splay, broken, in different directions. She wears a similar gown as Rebecca though her revealed flesh is pollen yellow and appears dappled upon her skin like a poor make-up job. Her head hangs down with chin against chest. Her eyes, black pits, stare into nowhere. Auburn hair hangs in mottled wet strips from a patchy scalp; exposed portions of her skull ooze with ochre-colored chemical burns.

On the flesh-wrapped bone of her left ring finger is a gold band with a small diamond-shaped stone in its center, black as obsidian.

She too weeps, but with great sadness.

Tears roll down the women's face, creep down cheek and chin, run off in small rivulets. The teardrops curl and wiggle as they fall upon the ladies clothing and to the floor, they pool into a mass of plump maggots at the women's feet. The awful larvae scuttle and squirm, disappearing from view as they slowly move—a tide of bloated inchworms—toward Jake's hospital bed.

Jake looks at Lettner. The man sits, smiling, as with knowledge of some as-of-yet unspoken triumph.

Before he can ask his question, the ex-NSC Commissioner answers it. "There's war coming, Captain, and you were so kind to accompany me on my final journey," a sinister grin curls the corners of Lettner's mouth almost to his ears, "I thought I'd accompany you... on yours."

GLOSSARY

HTV – Heavy Transport Vehicle

APC – Armored Personnel Carrier

BRV-O – Blast Resistant Vehicle-Off Road, a LTV to replace the Humvee

LTV – Light Tactical Vehicle

OP – Outpost, e.g. Bridge Street OP

GRCC – Grand Rapids Central Command

UCRA – Urban Civilian Retention Area, also Undead Civilian Retention Area (derogatory)

NSC – North Shore Coalition

BTF – Butterworth Test Facility

FZ – Feral Zombie

Peter Welmerink

HEAT round – High Explosive, Anti-Tank round

ZT or ZiT – Zombie Trooper

ROT – Rate of Fire

A-O, Alpha Oscar – "What's your A-O?" "What's your position?"

H7N9 – the strain of 2013 Bird Flu virus pandemic initiating the current zombie apocalypse

West Side Horde – a derogatory term for the UCRA citizens

SOWT – Special Operations Weather Technician

WOUNDED WARRIOR PROJECT

Zombie Troopers are fictional. Our wounded service men and women are not.

This author supports the Wounded Warrior Project. Will you?

http://www.woundedwarriorproject.org/

About the Author

Peter Welmerink was born and raised on the west side of pre-apocalyptic Grand Rapids, Michigan. He writes Fantasy, Military SciFi, and other wanderings into action-adventure. His work has been published in ye olde wood pulp print and electronic-online publications. He is the co-author of the Viking berserker novel, *BEDLAM UNLEASHED*, written with Steven Shrewsbury. *TRANSPORT* was his first solo novel venture. He is married with a small barbarian tribe of three boys.

Find out more about his works and upcoming projects at:
www.peterwelmerink.com

Transcend reality with Seventh Star Press!

On the following pages we would like to introduce you to some of our titles featuring Sword and Sorcery, Post-Apocalyptic Fantasy, Epic Fantasy, YA Fantasy, and more!

To get more information on Seventh Star Press and our titles, please visit:

www.seventhstarpress.com

or connect with us at:
www.twitter.com/7thstarpress
www.facebook.com/seventhstarpress

Now Available from Seventh Star Press,
the horror stylings of
Michael West!

Trade Paperback ISBN: 9780983740209
eBook ISBN: 9780983740216

Trade Paperback ISBN: 9781937929718
eBook ISBN: 9781937929725

Trade Paperback ISBN: 9781937929954
eBook ISBN:9781937929831

Trade Paperback ISBN: 978-1-937929-18-3
eBook ISBN: 978-1-937929-19-0

Begin the Adventures of Blue Shaefer in *Haunting Blue* from R.J. Sullivan!

Softcover ISBN: 978-1-941706-05-3
eBook ISBN: 978-1-941706-06-0

"She's discovered the town's biggest secret..... now there's hell to pay!"

Punk, blue-haired "Blue" Shaefer, is at odds with her workaholic single mother. Raised as a city girl in a suburb of Indianapolis, Blue must abandon the life she knows when her unfeeling mother moves them to a dreadful small town. Blue befriends the only student willing to talk to her: computer nerd "Chip" Farren.

Chip knows the connection between the rickety pirate boat ride at the local amusement park and the missing money from an infamous bank heist the townspeople still talk about. When Blue helps him recover the treasure, they awaken a vengeful ghost who'll stop at nothing–not even murder–to prevent them from exposing the truth behind his evil deeds.

Haunting Blue is Book One of the Adventures of Blue Shaefer

Urban Fantasy from John F. Allen!
Meet Ivory Blaque!

Softcover: 978-1-937929-16-9
eBook: 978-1-937929-17-6

In The God Killers, the first book of The God Killers Legacy, former professional art thief Ivory Blaque is hired to procure a pair of antique pistols and gets much more than she bargained for when several attempts are made on her life.

Her client turns out to be a shadowy government agent who reveals that she is descended from a race of immortals, and that the pistols are linked to her unique heritage and the special psychic gifts she possesses. He uses the memory of her father to guilt her into working for him.

Ivory eventually gives in to his request, and in return, he presents her with her father's journal, which was written in an unbreakable code. Bishop believes that she is the only one capable of breaking the code and unlocking the plans of the vampire hierarchy. But when the city's top vampire is a sexy incubus with an attraction for her and she's assigned a hot new lycan enforcer to protect her, she finds herself caught between two sets of rock hard abs.

To regain her autonomy, clear her name, unlock the secrets of her past, and protect the lives of those closest to her, Ivory must play along with the forces trying to manipulate her. Ivory's life is rapidly spiraling out of control and headed for an explosive conclusion which she just might not survive.

From Bram Stoker Award-winning Editor Michael Knost!

Softcover ISBN:
978-1-937929-61-9
eBook ISBN:
978-1-937929-62-6

Writers Workshop of Science Fiction and Fantasy is a collection of essays and interviews by and with many of the movers-and-shakers in the industry. Each contributor covers the specific element of craft he or she excels in. Expect to find varying perspectives and viewpoints, which is why you many find differing opinions on any particular subject.

This is, after all, a collection of advice from professional storytellers. And no two writers have made it to the stage via the same journey-each has made his or her own path to success. And that's one of the strengths of this book. The reader is afforded the luxury of discovering various approaches and then is allowed to choose what works best for him or her.

Featuring essays and interviews with:
Neil Gaiman, Orson Scott Card, Ursula K. Le Guin, Alan Dean Foster, James Gunn, Tim Powers, Harry Turtledove, Larry Niven, Joe Haldeman, Kevin J. Anderson, Elizabeth Bear, Jay Lake, Nancy Kress, George Zebrowski, Pamela Sargent, Mike Resnick, Ellen Datlow, James Patrick Kelly, Jo Fletcher, Stanley Schmidt, Gordon Van Gelder, Lou Anders, Peter Crowther, Ann VanderMeer, Joh Joseph Adams, Nick Mamatas, Lucy A. Snyder, Alethea Kontis, Nisi Shawl, Jude-Marie Green, Nayad A. Monroe, G. Cameron Fuller, Jackie Gamber, Amanda DeBord, Max Miller, Jason Sizemore.

Shadows Over Somerset from Bob Freeman!

Softcover: 978-1-941706-11-4
eBook: 978-1-941706-12-1

Michael Somers is brought to Cairnwood, an isolated manor in rural Indiana, to sit at the deathbed of a grandfather he never knew existed. He soon finds himself drawn into a strange and esoteric world filled with werewolves, vampires, witches... and a family curse that dates back to fourteenth century Scotland. In the sleepy little town of Somerset, an ancient evil awakens, hungering for blood and vengeance... and if Michael is to survive he must face his inner demons and embrace his family's dark past. Shadows Over Somerset is the first Cairnwood Manor Novel.

Appalachian Gothic! Jason Sizemore's Irredeemable!
18 Tales of dark fantasy, science fiction, and horror

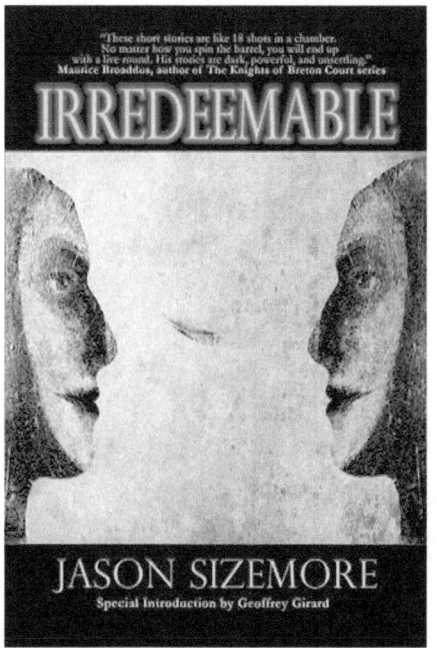

Softcover: 978-1-937929-59-6
eBook: 978-1-937929-68-8

Flowing like mists and shadows through the Appalachian Mountains come 18 tales from the mind of Jason Sizemore. Weaving together elements of southern gothic, science fiction, fantasy, horror, the supernatural, and much more, this diverse collection of short stories brings you an array of characters who must face accountability, responsibility, and, more ominously, retribution.

Whether it is Jack Taylor readying for a macabre, terrifying night in "The Sleeping Quartet," the Wayne brothers and mischief gone badly awry in "Pranks," the title character in "The Dead and Metty Crawford," or the church congregation and their welcoming of a special visitor in "Yellow Warblers," Irredeemable introduces you to a range of ordinary people who come face to face with extraordinary situations.

Whether the undead, aliens, ghosts, or killers of the yakuza, dangers of all kinds lurk within the darkness for those who dare tread upon its ground. Hop aboard and settle in, Irredeemable will take you on an unforgettable ride along a dark speculative fiction road.

A Horror Anthology from
Editors Alexander S. Brown and Louise Myers!

Softcover: 978-1-937929-54-1
eBook: 978-1-937929-64-0

From the fiery abyss of the underworld comes 20 hellish tales from the south and southwest. Within these charred pages are stories that will introduce you to the many demons that stay hidden but are always nearby…

20 authors provide stories of possessed people, objects, houses, highways, and the devil's favorite playground - the forest.

Dare to meet Deidless, a demon who is a buyer of souls. Discover what kind of demons men can summon. Read of battles between good and evil. Learn of ancient artifacts and stones that crave sacrifice. Finally, become acquainted with legions of evil.

Again, we invite you, sit back, dim the lights, and prepare yourself to meet the devils in the darkness.

Southern Haunts: Devils in the Darkness is the next in the exciting anthology series that began with Southern Haunts: Spirits That Walk Among Us.

www.ingramcontent.com/pod-product-compliance
Lightning Source LLC
Chambersburg PA
CBHW020614250626
47154CB00004B/1501